THE HERETIC'S SON

The Heretic's Son
The Assassins of Harmony: Book Three
Copyright © 2022 by Jamie McNabb
All rights reserved

Cover design by Allyson Longueira
Map design by Brandon Swann
Cover art copyright © Roberto Atzeni | Dreamstime.com

Ebook ISBN: 978-1-948447-17-1
Trade Paperback ISBN: 978-1-948447-18-8

Published by Soapbox Rising Press

The Heretic's Son

The Assassins of Harmony: Book Three

Jamie McNabb

Soapbox Rising Press

The Metropolitanate of The Inland Empire and The Holy Oregon

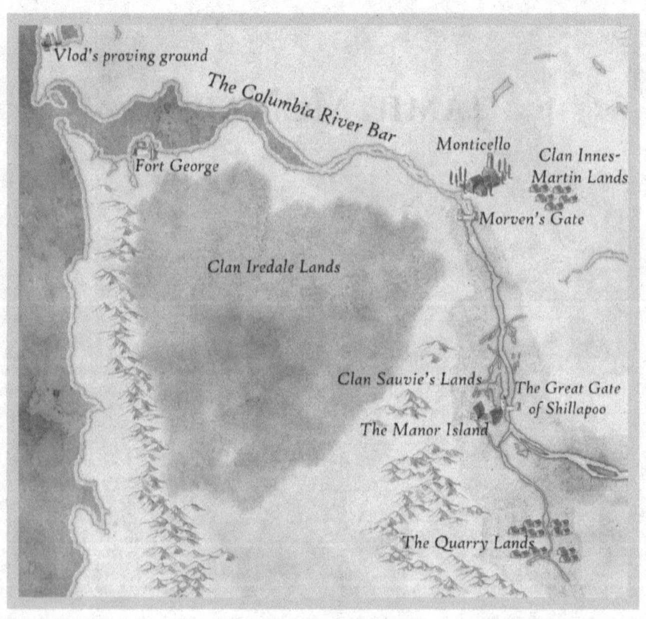

Lower Columbia River

THE METROPOLITANATE OF THE INLAND EMPIRE AND THE HOLY OREGON

Upper Columbia River

ONE

Even before *Morning Victor*'s mooring lines had been secured, Wolfram's messenger leapt across from the dock. He seized whatever handholds and footholds he could find, and grinning broadly, he scrambled up the side. He vaulted over the bulwark, and onto the deck.

He had a spidery build, red hair, and skin that would never tan. It would burn and it would peel, but it would never tan. His teeth were white and fairly straight, no obvious rot.

"You're in one hell of a hurry," the captain groused.

The grin widened.

This wasn't a wise move on the messenger's part.

The captain bellowed, "You could have fallen! You could have been crushed between the ship and the dock!"

"Yes, sir."

"Any idea who'd end up scraping you off the side of the hull with a spatula?"

"No, sir."

"My crew would."

"Yes, sir."

"You're a damn fool and a fucking showoff."

"Sorry, sir."

"Don't 'Sorry, sir' me, you little shit! State your fucking business and then get the hell off of my ship, you selfish moron!"

"Yes, sir."

The message was to the point: Wolfram, Clan Iredale's battlemaster sent his compliments to the captain and asked him to instruct Brenna and Vlod to stay aboard and await his arrival.

In return, via the captain, Brenna and Vlod sent their respects to Wolfram and said they'd be glad to await his arrival.

By this time the ship was secure alongside and the gangway was over.

Standing at the top of the gangway, the messenger waved at the captain. "Welcome back, Grandad. See you tonight for dinner."

"If you live that long," the captain said.

The messenger went ashore, and the captain went below.

To Brenna, Vlod said, "Reminds me of you and your uncle, way back when."

"I lived long enough to grow up, didn't I?"

"We both have," Vlod said.

"No thanks to Ulricka," Brenna said.

Vlod made a dismissive gesture. "She's trapped and looking for a way out. It's bound to throw out the odd misstep."

Brenna made a noncommittal noise. "He's read our reports."

"That's why we sent them on ahead, wasn't it?" Vlod said.

"Your girlish optimism is wearing a trifle thin," Brenna said.

"I do my best to curb it."

"No you don't," she said. She added, "The dispatch riders must have made good time."

"Clever boys, and they're good riders."

"We'll have the devil to pay and no pitch hot."

"Never fear," Vlod said. "Hot pitch will be provided."

"Buckets and buckets of it."

"And a mop, too."

A half hour later, Wolfram slid in behind the captain's worktable and sat on the stern locker. The glare from the windows threw his face into deep shadow. He smelled like leather, oiled steel, and tobacco smoke.

"I'll talk to you later, Brenna," Wolfram said. "Please wait outside and see that Vlod and I are not disturbed."

"I'd rather stay. It was my operation as much as his."

Wolfram slammed his palm down onto the tabletop. The report was deafening in the confined space. "Out!"

"Aye, aye, sir," Brenna said, and left.

To Vlod, Wolfram said, "You've nearly started a war."

Vlod shrugged. It was the response he'd expected, and he had his response rehearsed. "Narmer started it months ago. All I've done, the most I've done, is to force it out into the open."

"Maybe so, you arrogant puppy, but we're not ready for an open war. You've given them an excuse to attack us at will."

"By rescuing Royden?"

"Exactly."

"I thought you sent me upriver to do precisely that."

"I didn't send you up there to pick a fight with the Cathedral Guard!"

"No picking was involved."

"Tell that to the dead!"

Vlod sighed. Beneath the rage and disappointment, Wolfram was frightened. Rightly so. Vlod said, "Narmer seized Royden illegally, and Ulricka took possession of him illegally. We had every right to free him by any and all means necessary."

"*Illegally* be damned. You can't be that stupid. It's the overall look of the thing. It's about the politics. The minor clans don't give a damn about legal niceties."

"About what then?" The question was unnecessary, but Vlod had to ask it. He had to know exactly what the battlemaster was thinking and why.

"What they'll care about is that you stormed in and freed one of Ulricka's prisoners," Wolfram said. "Never mind that she was holding him illegally. That's beside the point. Or had you thought that far ahead? What they'll care about is that you attacked her forces and left several of her people dead. What they'll care about even more is that you violated the sovereignty of their precious cathedral and their revered Mother Metropolitan."

"Meaning?"

"Meaning that you've handed Narmer the perfect pretext."

"Narmer doesn't give a shit about pretexts," Vlod said.

"Perhaps not, but Ulricka does and the clans do. They have an obsessive need to appear as though they're acting within the right."

Where was the right in allowing Narmer to kidnap one of the magi assigned to Clan Iredale?

Vlod had better sense than to pose the question. The clans saw to clan business, and the magi saw to magi business. The overlap muddied the waters in this case, but so be it.

Instead of going down that road, Vlod asked, "Where do things stand here at the manor? What about the project?"

"Edmund and I have shut it down. Call it another casualty of your lack of anticipation."

***

Edmund and Royden paced along the battlements above Olney Castle's western gate. The sky was clear and the sun shone down as though it were summer instead of spring.

"What did you find out?" Edmund asked.

They had already been through Royden's kidnapping, his treatment at the hands of Narmer's people, his handling at the hands of Ulricka's people, his rescue, Vlod's presentation of the appeal, and what had followed.

Now they were down to whether or not Royden had accomplished his mission, his mission within the mission. What had he ferreted out about the cathedral, about Ulricka's court?

Royden said, "They're a tight-lipped bunch. Touch-me-not to the core. Their wear their piety on their sleeves. No dissatisfaction with Her Beatitude that I could detect, but I did hear a healthy amount of grumbling. They aren't afraid, they're not what I'd call unsettled, but they are aware that not everything is as it should be."

Edmund and Royden reached a corner, rounded it, and walked along the south battlement. The upper reaches of Young's Bay lay spread out at the base of the hill. Farther out, the view presented a patchwork of fields, the bay, Young's River, tide flats, marshes, a winding road, commercial oyster beds, and a scattering of small buildings.

Edmund asked, "What about Narmer?"

"My guess would be that he has agents up and down the bureaucracy."

"How many?"

"Not above a half dozen, but from what I could tell, they're in the right places."

"Is Ulricka aware of them?"

"Yes, and she's worried about them, too. I could tell as much from the questions Narmer's agents asked me."

The sun's warmth was reassuring after the winter they'd had. In the rain-soaked darkness of December, January, and February, day after day of what amounted to twilight, it was second nature to fear that the days would never lengthen again, that spring and summer would never return.

Every year the same question made its unspoken, unacknowledged rounds: Had the Goddess decided to perform a Third Creation? Let there be darkness!

"What about the Cathedral Guard? Compromised or not?"

"No idea. Narmer may have infiltrated it. He'd be a fool not to. Easy enough, too, as far as I could tell. It's wide open."

A cloud passed in front of the sun, and the day turned dark and cold. It was an aftertaste of winter.

Two

Less than a week after *Morning Victor*'s return, Shabnan, the Crone of the Cathedral, landed in Fort George. She had traveled downriver aboard the second of the Nebti, *The Eyes of Wadjet*, and had demanded an immediate audience with Edmund and Vernon.

Edmund had sent a rider, and Vernon, Trevor, and a small guard had arrived from Monticello, the Innes-Martin capital, two days later.

Now, with the seven people crowded into Edmund's study, with the coffee poured and the small talk behind them, Shabnan put the Cathedral's business on the table. It had to do with the rockets that Vlod, Aerian, and Desmond had been working on.

Vlod sat with his hands empty, his cup sitting on the floor next to his chair.

A low fire was burning on the grate, a holdover from the morning, which had been cold and wet. Between the fire and the overcrowding, the room was stuffy and uncomfortably warm.

Brenna had opened a window, and the fresh air was helping, but it was helping less than Vlod would have liked.

What he would have liked would have been to flee, to wake up and discover that he had only dreamed that Shabnan had imposed herself, that her arrival had been a passing nightmare.

Edmund said, "As I've been trying to explain, we've halted the work."

"I'm glad to hear it," Shabnan said. She sounded neither glad nor convinced.

"It's over and done with," Edmund said.

"It may be over, but it's far from done with," Shabnan said.

Seeming to brush aside the threat, Edmund sipped his coffee. "They stumbled into weaponization inadvertently. I found out about it, and now I've put a stop to it. They're back on track: improvements to signaling rockets."

"We could use better signaling rockets," Vernon said. "This section of the river can turn surprisingly dangerous, often without any warning."

Shabnan glared at him.

Had Vernon, Vlod wondered, threatened her safety? Or had he been stating a fact of life on the lower Columbia. Conditions could deteriorate in an instant. A midday pleasure cruise could change into a life-or-death struggle within a matter of seconds: groundings, collisions, fires, deadheads, deteriorating weather. The list was endless.

Shabnan returned her attention to Edmund. "The fact that you've abandoned work you shouldn't have undertaken in the first place won't extricate you."

"Extricate me from *what*?" Edmund demanded.

The Crone had traveled down from the Cathedral to bludgeon Edmund and Vernon into submission, into accepting Ulricka's rejection of their appeal. They were *not* to challenge her. They were not to find other grounds and appeal a second time.

True, the rockets were a serious matter, a clear violation of dozens of tenants, but in essence, at this juncture, they were window dressing, a thinly veiled excuse.

Edmund said, "I'm not the one who's violated the terms of my sacred office."

Vernon nodded in agreement. "Did Ulricka even read our appeal of Warrick's ruling?"

"She read it," Shabnan said.

No one had bothered to ask Vlod, who had, after all, been in the room when Ulricka had scrawled her rejection.

"As a partisan," Vernon said, "but not as a neutral judge. Warrick had no grounds, he—"

Edmund jumped in. "I'm not the one who's dancing on the edge of a public charge of malfeasance."

"With a layer of wet ice on the dance floor," Vernon said.

Wolfram, Trevor, Brenna, and Vlod remained mute.

Vlod refused himself the pleasure of a slight grin. The combination of metaphors didn't quite match. Edges and dancefloor. Then again, dancefloors did have edges, and if Ulricka overstepped she would find herself a wallflower.

Meanwhile, Shabnan was making no effort to hide her contempt for the boys and their insignificant displeasure. "Malfeasance?"

"She's violating her own neutrality," Edmund said.

"How's that?"

"She's failing to adjudicate a legitimate appeal in an open and disinterested manner, favoring neither one side nor the other," Edmund said. "Her ruling wasn't based on the evidence, exactly as Warrick's wasn't. An interesting coincidence, that."

Shabnan's contempt hardened. "You wouldn't be complaining if she'd ruled in your favor." Her contempt became open scorn.

Another emotion was in play as well. At first, Vlod couldn't name it, but it was akin to embarrassment. Events had exposed Ulricka's machinations, her incompetence, and her cowardice.

Shabnan, Ulricka's loyal counselor and protector, had to be going through an unparalleled flood of *shame*. Yes, that was the word: *shame*.

Edmund said, "I ended the rocketry project as an act of good faith. It's time for Ulricka to reciprocate."

It was one of Edmund's better rejoinders. Without histrionics, he had made his position clear: If Ulricka did not return to a position of absolute political and military neutrality, Edmund would resume work on gunpowder-fired weaponry.

Shabnan said, "Not good enough. You must destroy the research and hand over the magi Vlod, Royden, Aerian, and Desmond for trial. You must also surrender control of the mouth of the Columbia River to a commission of chieftains headed by the Mother Metropolitan herself. You must also pay an indemnity. Otherwise, Her Beatitude will line the hilltops with burning heretics."

"How dramatic!" Brenna said. "Can we roast sausages?"

Wolfram guffawed, but Trevor remained blank-faced, a man of no expression, giving nothing away.

One thing was clear, however. Ulricka's demands proved the extent of Narmer's control over the cathedral. Further, they proved that he was hoping to start a war.

In that light, perhaps they betrayed the extent of Ulricka's fear of the man.

Vernon said, "If anyone's likely to light up a hilltop, it's Ricki." And with that, he handed Shabnan his and Vernon's appeal of Ulricka's ruling, freshly drafted and sealed with their seals in the finest wax.

Shabnan was not pleased.

Wind-driven rain stung Vlod's face.

Shabnan's ship, *The Eyes of Wadjet*, backed away from the terminal. She made her turn and headed out into the channel. She passed Buoy 40, turned upriver, and set her sails.

Edmund returned to Olney Castle, but Wolfram and Vlod stayed behind.

The rain was drifting down now, now that the worst of the squall line had passed through. The rain billowed like a cold, heavy mist. The droplets soaked through Vlod's cloak. The cloak ought to have kept him dry, but it didn't.

"Shall I restart the project?" Vlod asked.

"The rockets, you mean? No. Vernon wouldn't put up with them. You ought to have heard the howling when we explained what you and the boys had been up to. You'd have thought you were trying to reintroduce firearms."

Vlod shivered. "I don't understand," he said. "You pointed us at the rockets because weaponized rockets are a military necessity...or soon will be."

"Yes, and now they're a political liability. We need a miracle, not smoke and noise."

THREE

April eased into May. The coming summer was not to be rushed, but the balance between rain and sun was shifting in favor of sunny days. The bouts of rain shortened, seemed less intense, almost gentle. The days lengthened. The cherry and dogwood trees bloomed. The rhododendrons exploded in unimaginably rich colors, reds and purples, pinks and whites. Rather than smelling of damp and rot and mud, the air was heady with the aromas of evergreens, flowers, Scotch broom, fish-drying racks, smoking meat, new-sawn lumber, and newly tilled farmland.

The Mother Metropolitan's herald rode up to the main gate of Edmund's castle. The gate was open, but he did not enter. He dismounted in one unhurried movement, like an avalanche that was taking its own sweet time. He was a man of no mean skill, then.

His uniform was white. His horse was white. The paper he took from his dispatch pouch was white. He was to be seen as a pure man on a pure errand.

An old man on the road outside the gate paused to watch. He observed to himself that white was indeed the color of purity, but that it was also the color of burial shrouds. White was the color of death. Was the dispatch rider, then, a pale rider?

A detachment from the Cathedral Guard, unmistakable in their uniforms, fanned out in a protective formation around the herald. Their horses were bays; their uniforms were leather and linen, in black and white, with purple accents. They had death's head devices on their hats. Hussars, then. Yellow, white, and purple streamers flew from their lances. The hilts of their sabers sparkled like wavelets in the sun. The tassels were gold, black, and white, made of tightly woven silk.

The herald was indeed a pale rider.

He was as pale as pale could be.

A harbinger of death if the rumors were true.

The castle gates stood open, and people hurried in and out. Like the old man, they stared at the herald, but unlike the old man, they walked on by. What was another popinjay to them? They had work to do. They had baking to deliver. They had cloth to weave, horses to shoe, wheat to mill, leather to tan, logs to saw, and wood to cook into charcoal.

The herald brought out a hammer and nails. The hammer was not white. It was steel and the color of steel. The nails were also of steel, a blackish gray.

The herald nailed the white paper to the gate.

The paper's black border made its meaning clear. Black, the old man noted, was the color of grief, the color of sin, the color of woe, the color of death. The text confirmed it: the Mother Metropolitan had declared a jihad—a holy war, a crusade—against Edmund, Vernon, their clans, and all those allied with them.

Madness!

The old man fingered the pommel of his battle knife, remembering and wondering. It was a good knife, one that held its edge. He kept it well oiled. It had a snarling lion's head on the pommel and scrollwork on the guard. He thought about the lion, and then he walked on.

Four

A cold day, it's logic unrelenting.

Spring or not, midday or not, a fitful wind whipped across the proving ground, far out on the Long Beach Peninsula. The wind ruffled the grass and lashed the tall weeds back and forth. The air was cold and wet and smelled of muddy sand. Off to the east, Willapa Bay was dark gray. Its color matched the low-hanging clouds. Dilatory, short-lived whitecaps flecked the surface of the water.

Vlod ripped the "Keep Out" sign from the tent flap and cut the security lashings.

His time was short. He'd bluffed his way past the sentries, but by now they'd have come to their senses and raised an alarm...or soon would. Their sergeant would arrive in a matter of minutes. Five at the outside.

Vlod hurried into the work tent.

Weeks ago, the clan's battlemaster had sent a detail to take possession of critical documents and to secure the work site.

Well and good, but how much had Wolfram's people saved, and how much had they left behind? Later on, how much had others looted or vandalized? How much had been carried away for souvenirs?

How much that could be of any possible use had been left behind?

Vlod pulled away the tarp covering the nearest worktable.

Surprisingly, the tools were in place, and the work-in process laid out. A rocket fin remained clamped in the vise.

However, there wasn't a scrap of paper to be seen: no folders, no notes, no designs, no notebooks, no measurements.

Vlod looked around.

What would have Wolfram done with the papers the project had generated?

He'd have tucked them away in Olney Castle.

Fine, but where?

Would he give them to Vlod, or would he pretend that he'd destroyed them?

No, Wolfram wouldn't—

The tent flap flew open and a marine captain burst in.

"What do you think you're doing?" he demanded.

"My duty," Vlod said. He stepped closer to the officer, challenging him to strike. Rather than explaining himself, Vlod said, "Send runners to the magi Aerian and Desmond. They are to join me here immediately. Tell them we have a job to finish."

———

A couple of days after Vlod's return to the proving ground, Edmund, his ears ringing from what had been reported to him, went in search of his brother, Wolfram, the clan's battlemaster, a man who ought to have known better than to play fast and loose with the Cathedral.

Edmund found him down by the river, in the midst of a landing exercise.

Edmund drew his horse up next to his brother.

"You don't look any too happy," Wolfram commented.

"I'm not."

Several meters away, on one of the broader river beaches, men-at-arms beached their boats and scrambled ashore through a hail of dummy arrows. Ink-soaked balls of cloth tipped the shafts.

Those without ink marks were deemed to have survived. Those with ink marks were deemed to have perished in the landing.

Given the high proportion of men-at-arms with ink on their

dummy uniforms, the landing could only be judged to be a humiliating failure. It would be announced as such as soon as the marshals ended the farce.

The sooner the better.

There is only so much humiliation an army could be expected to endure.

Wolfram pointed at a boat that had been dragged up onto the sand. Around it lolled about a dozen men. They were alternatively playing dice and watching the exercise. The coxswain lounged next to the boat's tiller, his feet propped on the gunwale. Being dead was hard work.

"The defenders wiped out the Number Five Boat's crew and landing party," Wolfram explained.

"You're with me," Edmund said, and spurred his horse from the beach.

Wolfram wheeled his mount around. "Where are we off to?"

"To clean up one of your messes."

<hr>

At the sound of approaching riders, Vlod and Aerian looked up from their work.

At the head of a small military column, Edmund and Wolfram rode onto the proving ground.

Vlod set a tinderbox within reach of a launch tube. A spider-work of adjustable supports held the tube at a steep upward angle. The whole contraption stood as high as the top of Vlod's head. A rocket, ready to fire, sat inside the tube.

"They're sooner than I expected," Vlod commented.

"Any soon is too soon," Aerian said. "How's the food in jail?"

"Roasted over an open fire," Vlod said.

"We're not on the menu."

"Yet."

"Have they found Desmond, do you think? Is that why they've come?"

Vlod lifted a marine-grade, pocket telescope to his eye and scanned the riders. Wolfram. Edmund. Men-at-arms. But no Desmond. "They didn't bring him," Vlod said. "Keep on working. I'll stall them until you're ready."

"No problem," Aerian said.

"Remember, nothing succeeds like success."

"One of Gluth's aphorisms?"

"Well, it's on a sign in his tavern."

Aerian didn't have a lot to do to finish preparing the rocket. In that sense, Edmund and Wolfram's arrival was a bit of luck. Nevertheless, Aerian made a point of doing what little he had to do. Perhaps fate had taken a turn. It was a comforting thought. Silly, but comforting.

Not so silly, either, now that he came to think about it.

The riders arrived and dismounted, except for two archers, who remained pointedly mounted, their bows and quivers comfortably within reach.

Rather than glare menacingly, the archers smiled as though they were anticipating a round of target practice.

Edmund told the two magi he'd come to arrest them for insubordination. What did they have to say?

Aerian apologized for being insubordinate, but he kept busy with the rocket.

Vlod said they were at a critical stage and couldn't leave off. They'd be happy to be arrested—honored in fact—but that right now wasn't a good time.

Wolfram did his best not to laugh out loud, but the archer's smiles widened.

"You'll do as you're told," Edmund said.

Four men-at-arms strode forward, dividing themselves between Vlod and Aerian.

Two each.

Vlod shifted his weight slightly.

Two?

Child's play.

"My lord," Vlod said, "the project was—"

"I'm finished!" Aerian announced. "It's ready!"

He moved away from the rocket, only to be seized by the men-at-arms who'd approached him.

A dodge, a twist, two sharp blows and the men-at-arms were on the ground, dazed but otherwise undamaged. A spin and a forearm block sent an archer's arrow tumbling away.

The two who'd approached Vlod had better sense than to lay hands on him.

"My lord, please," Vlod said. "Have your men stand down. Otherwise, someone is going to end up hurt."

Wolfram made a casual gesture. Bows were lowered, and people relaxed.

"Just who in hell do you think you are?" Edmund demanded.

Rather than argue, Vlod snatched up the tinderbox and lit the rocket's fuse.

"Cover your ears, my lord," Vlod said.

Five minutes later, Wolfram scooped up a handful of sand from the place where the rocket had landed and *exploded*.

The rocket had done its job, or near enough.

The immediate prospect of jail was off the table, but the four men-at-arms had not yet returned to their horses, nor had the archers returned their bows to their saddle scabbards.

Wolfram sniffed at his handful of sand, made a face, and dropped the sand back onto the blackened ground. He gazed at a square of canvas stretched between two poles off to his right, the ostensible target. It was a few meters distant, not many, but a few, untouched and unharmed. "You missed," he said.

"Guidance is a problem," Vlod said, "but—"

"Maybe not," Edmund said.

"My lord?" Vlod asked.

Just as Wolfram had done, Edmund scooped up a handful of sand from the site of the detonation. "Fire enough of those into an enemy formation and you're bound to open up a hole. Open up enough of them, and they'll break." As Wolfram had, he sniffed at the sand. He made a face and dropped it. "Smelly sons of bitches, your *improved* signaling rockets."

"It's part of their inimitable charm," Wolfram said.

"Smells like the doorway to hell," Edmund said.

"Noise and smoke won't panic them for long," Wolfram said.

"How long would we need?"

It was a largely rhetorical question.

"Long enough to lop heads," Wolfram said.

Edmund grimaced. He and his brother had radically different ideas about war. As far as Edmund was concerned, he'd won the battle the moment the enemy quit the field. Wolfram refused to count a battle as having been won until he had either taken prisoner or killed the very last enemy soldier.

With a nod, Edmund dismissed the four men-at-arms and the two archers.

When the six were safely out of earshot, Edmund turned to Vlod. "How many rockets can you build and how quickly can you build them?"

"How soon?" Vlod asked.

"Soon."

"Not enough to win a war. We have hundreds of problems left to solve, especially when—"

"I don't expect perfection. I expect useable."

"Yes, my lord."

"Tell me what you need."

Vlod looked back uprange at the empty launch tube, then at the construction tent. When he'd fired the rocket, the horses had reared and skittered as though they were on anthills. When the device had detonated, the problem had redoubled: rolling eyes, rearing, and attempts to run away. In battle, untrained horses were sure to panic. The resulting chaos would be as deadly as any weapon.

But that didn't answer the core questions.

How many rockets would it take to reduce an army to a terrified mob? A score? Two score? A hundred?

And which type would have the greater effect: a dozen big ones or scores of smaller ones?

"I'll need the return of our papers," Vlod said.

"Done," Wolfram said.

"What else?" Edmund asked.

"Construction materials and workmen."

"Send me a requisition," Edmund said. "What else?"

"Mostly, we'll need time and secrecy," Vlod said. "My lord, if you want to defeat Narmer, you must buy us the time to produce the means."

"Secrecy," Wolfram said, drawing out the word. "The minor chieftains cannot learn what we're up to. As long as it's rumors, we can deny them."

"What about Vernon?" Edmund asked.

Wolfram made a face, then made another. "We'll have to tell him. I'll have a private word with Trevor, plant a rumor in his ear, if you take my meaning. That way Vernon can always claim we kept him in the dark."

"Agreed," Edmund said. "I'll open negotiations with Ulricka. She'd rather gloat than hand Narmer the whole of Lower Egypt.

The couriers sped up and down the river. When the flurry of messages was over, Edmund boarded *Koan*, his war galley, and pointed her bronze-shod ram upriver.

Seldon, the chieftain of Clan Sauvie, had volunteered to host a meeting between Edmund, Vernon, Ulricka, and Narmer. It was a fine idea, Edmund thought, but Seldon had demanded a gut-wrenching price in exchange for his good offices. He, too, would be taking part.

FIVE

Two days after Edmund's departure for New Boston, Seldon's capital and the jewel of Sauvie's Island, Brenna arrived on the Long Beach proving ground. She brought a work gang, two companies of marines, three supply wagons, and Desmond, much the worse for wear. His face was puffy and plaster white. Before dismounting, he leaned over and threw up.

He wiped his mouth on the back of his sleeve. To no one in particular, he said, "I hate fresh air, and I hate this fucking horse!"

The marines reported to the officer tasked with guarding the peninsula, and the work gang started unloading the wagons.

Brenna hooked a thumb at Desmond. "Look what I found."

"In a tavern or in a brothel?" Vlod asked.

As if to confirm Vlod's assessment, Desmond bent over, hands on knees, and vomited a second pearl-gray slurry onto the ground. He spat a couple of times, then righted himself into a slouch.

"Sorry," he said. His voice was raspy and loud, as though he were shouting across a noisy tavern. "I'm not as resilient as I used to be."

"I found him passed out in the Grove and Ax," Brenna said. "You sent for him, didn't you?"

"I must have had a reason," Vlod said.

The stench of alcohol-laced vomit slithered through the air around them.

"You can use him, though, can't you?" Brenna asked.

"Not until he's cleaned up."

Rather than enter New Boston's central mooring basin, a move that would have left *Koan* trapped inside the Great Gate of Shillapoo, Edmund chose to anchor outside in the river. If Seldon took offense, so be it.

Koan had sailed upstream with two escorts and five scouts. The scouts were fast, heavily armed open boats. They could sprint to wherever the squadron's commander needed them and strike as hard as necessary. The escorts were medium war galleys, fully decked, and mounted with catapults fore and aft. Taken together, *Koan* and her squadron were not to be underestimated.

Neither were the Sauvies. In addition to its mainland territories, Seldon's manor occupied Sauvie's Island.

The Manor Island, as it was also called, was nestled between the Little William, and a branch of the Little William called the Multnomah Channel (for reasons lost to history) and the Columbia River.

At its widest point, the island was a half-day's march from east to west, and at its longest point, it was a day's march from north to south. At the time of the Second Creation, shallow lakes, streams, and marshes occupied about a third of the area, but incredibly fertile farmland had made up the rest.

The first- and second-century Sauvies had been neither reckless nor stupid. Within a generation or two, they discovered they had nothing to gain, apart from annoyance and disease, from raising mosquitoes. They also discovered that farmland was a better survival tool than swampland.

Therefore, while cherishing their existing land, they hauled in dirt from the mainland and judiciously filled in most of the lakes, bogs, and low patches. They installed a network of windmill-driven pumps in order to keep the water table within bounds and the land arable.

A stone curtain wall surrounded the entire island, but the manor's crowning glory was the aptly named Great Gate of Shillapoo. The gate was a massive structure with battlements and permanently mounted throwing engines. Its steel and bronze-shod doors were as tall as most river barges were long.

Via a short canal, the gate opened into a broad mooring basin, deep even at the end of summer. That basin was the commercial heart of New Boston, their capitol. Warehouses, foundries, shops, mills, shipyards, and workshops ringed the docks and piers. Ships and barges from up and down the length of the river choked the docks and anchorages.

There was talk of building docks and warehouses outside the wall, on pilings and fill, the crush was so great.

Seldon's Hall, which was named not for the current occupant but for Seldon the Great, was the largest and oldest building in New Boston. The hall was not so much a keep, fortress, or castle, as it was a palace and administrative center. To be sure, there were the odd military touches—a curtain wall, the building's stone walls, arrow loops, steel shutters, internal cisterns and storerooms, and battlements—but by and large, the balance favored convenience, comfort, and aesthetics.

And why not? Clan Sauvie controlled enormous tracts of land in addition to the island, and the hall stood behind one defensive ring after another: two rivers; the island's curtain wall; the massive, steel-reinforced walls of the city of New Boston; and the hall's own curtain wall. The hall could afford to be expansive, to enjoy the luxury of an abundance of light and air.

Wolfram maintained that the island's defenses were nonsense. It was armies in the field that decided wars, not armies cowering behind walls. Stones did not fight wars. Walls were good against brigands and desultory attacks, but they could never prevail against determined armies equipped with proper siege engines, nor could they stand against the attentions of inventive sappers.

Sappers? In private, Seldon offered the opinion that Sauvie's Island had four moats: the Little William, the Multnomah Channel, the Columbia, and the island's own water table—unless his putative attacker commanded sappers who could breathe mud.

The parties to the negotiation held their opening session in a private dining room in the Hall's southeast tower. A low fire warded off the morning chill, oil lamps fought against the gloom of an overcast day, and the slightly opened windows dispelled the mustiness of habitual disuse.

Seldon the Great, the current Seldon's grandfather, had substantially remodeled and enlarged the Hall, but he had left the tower dining room untouched.

Several of the Hall's rooms and apartments had been formally named, complete with plaques, but the tower dining room had not. Rather straightforwardly it had never been called anything else.

The room had been Seldon the Great's favorite place to hold intimate meals and quiet negotiations, but the current Seldon abhorred its low ceilings, undressed-stone walls, and plank floors. He despised its carpets, which were worn, faded, patched, and garishly patterned in styles that favored flowers, vines, and symmetrical, geometric designs.

As much as he loathed them, he balked at changing them out. He often wondered what that said about him. He'd changed other things, countless other things. He was making his mark, determined to leave Clan Sauvie better off than it had been when he'd ascended to the chieftaincy. But every time he decided to get rid of those bits of rag on the floor, something stopped him.

The tower dining room, apart from the carpets, had its advantages. No few of them. Therefore, Seldon had chosen it because it was the right size, out of the way, and impossible to approach unseen. It was secure.

After Seldon had dismissed the servants, he closed and locked the doors. They were massive, ironbound brutes. There were six people in attendance. The first five—Edmund and Vernon, Ulricka and Narmer, and Seldon—had armies at their disposal. They had political and religious standing.

The sixth, Xenia, Seldon's sister, did not. Her purpose in being there was, she averred, "to fetch whatever needed fetching and to write down whatever needed writing down." She was the meek and humble servant of her great and powerful brother.

Edmund knew better. She had included herself in order to anchor her brother. Without her, he'd spin around like a weathercock in a thunderstorm, never pointing in the same direction for more than a few seconds at a time.

Narmer objected to her participation. Addressing Seldon directly, he asked, "How many troops does your sister command?"

Xenia answered for her brother. "How many henge dancers and priestesses do you command?"

The would-be pharaoh made a low-pitched sound of disgust as the implication of that question sank in. Armies might fight the wars, but it was the manor henges that provided the bedrock of moral sanction. Without it, no army would march.

Ulricka smiled, somewhat knowingly, somewhat sadly.

In Xenia, Edmund thought, Ulricka confronted an independent woman, a potential rival for power. Xenia lived outside Ulricka's orbit, outside her day-to-day control. As a chieftain's sister, as a henge dancer, Xenia understood the mechanisms of spiritual power, if not the minutiae of theology and cathedral politics.

Most dangerously to Ulricka, Xenia was free to act on whatever ambitions she might have. Xenia may have directed her jibe at Narmer, but she had, changing the changeable, meant it for Ulricka: *Don't fuck with me, honey. I was born to play political games, and you weren't.*

"She stays," Ulricka said. "Voice but no vote."

"Voice *and* vote or we call it off," Vernon said.

Edmund cocked an eyebrow. He'd received a report detailing Xenia's impromptu visit to Vernon's manor. A hunting trip gone bad? Eyewash! Ten-to-one said that his brother chieftain had plowed—was plowing?— that island field.

Narmer glared at Vernon, while at the same time, Seldon's face contorted as though he were about to experience an explosive bowel movement.

Ulricka said, "Very well, if it pleases you. Voice *and* vote."

With that rigmarole behind them, Seldon formally welcomed his guests. It was a nice little speech. He expressed his hope for a successful outcome to their talks. He pleaded for mutual patience, tolerance, and understanding. He promised to make everyone's stay as comfortable and as enjoyable as possible.

He passed the floor to Ulricka.

The Mother Metropolitan proclaimed the need for mutual trust, the imperative for courageous leadership, the duty to join the divinely inspired quest for peace, the universal duty to serve and guard the Harmony, and the universal obligation to stamp out heresy and deviationism. She reinforced the overriding needs, first, for a stable and lasting peace and, second, for correct religious belief and practice. Heresy was as dangerous to the wellbeing of the Inland Empire and the Holy Oregon as were unlicensed technological innovation and open warfare.

Edmund asked her, "Are you and I at war or not? You declared a jihad against us, but our armies haven't engaged. In fact, we're here talking. I'm confused."

"Why have you and Vernon deployed your forces so far upstream?" Ulricka asked.

"My forces are on my side of my eastern border. They have not crossed into neutral territory."

"Nor have mine," Vernon added. "Unlike your friend here—" he gestured toward Narmer "—my army is on my own ground."

Narmer threw himself so far forward he nearly rose out of his chair. He struck the tabletop with his fist. "My forces escort the Mother Metropolitan!"

"And therein lies a tale," Vernon said.

"What about the Cathedral Guard?" Edmund asked. "Isn't it their role to protect the Mother Metropolitan?"

To Narmer, Xenia said, "Do you intend to imply that my brother and I are a threat to Her Beatitude?"

"You do not control the entire length of the river," Narmer said.

"I agree with Edmund," Xenia said. "The Mother Metropolitan has her own forces. They ought to be escorting her."

"I brought my own detachment," Ulricka said. "They're adequate to the task. I came downriver with Narmer out of convenience rather than necessity."

It was an interesting comment, fierce in its way. It cut the props out from under Narmer's claim that he was guarding her and it put him in his place, or at least into the place Ulricka wished them to believe he occupied.

"My forces are here as a precaution," Narmer said. "These are dangerous times. Who can say how large an attacking force might be?"

Edmund stared at the would-be pharaoh as if he were a dog that had misbehaved.

Narmer stared back at him.

The Iredale chieftain found it difficult not to turn away in revulsion. Narmer was stupefyingly ugly. He had a round sweaty face and a stubby, bulbous nose. His eyes and mouth were too small for his watermelon head.

In the end, it was Narmer who looked away.

Not a good sign in a would-be conqueror.

Of Ulricka, Edmund asked, "How are we to determine, from the outside, whether or not you remain in command of the jihad you have declared?"

SIX

Edmund watched the fire in the fireplace of his suite's sitting room. Seldon had offered the rooms, which had a view of the Inner Harbor, and Edmund had accepted them. It would have been rude not to.

The day's sessions were long over, the evening banquet was recently over, and his talks with Wolfram and Vernon were just over. The odors of the two men—consisting of oiled steel for Wolfram and brushed horses for Vernon—lingered in the room. Otherwise, the space smelled of wood smoke from the fire, of pitch from the wood stacked in the wood rack, of smoke from the lamp, of disuse, of mildew, of a woman's perfume, and, faintly, at a distance, of rats.

Taken as a whole, the room was small but comfortable. Most of the tapestries featured hunting scenes, but Seldon had bestowed pride of place to a depiction of Eileen the Immortal's iconic and seminal *Discourse at Warrior Rock*.

It had been at Warrior Rock that Eileen, a Sauvie, had first preached the Second Creation and the transcendence of the Harmony, there that she had raised the First Jihad against the forces of patriarchal superstition and spiritual deviationism, there that she had revealed the grotesque horror of mindless technological innovation, there that she had

26

unleashed the relentless destruction and demolition of the surviving remnants and exemplars of humanity's industrial and postindustrial technologies.

Her discourse had also signaled the beginning of the end for the surviving remnants of Christianity, Judaism, Buddhism, Hinduism, Islam, and countless others, and it had motivated the extermination of the shamanic, druidic, cave, forest, and cauldron cults that had taken root during the Great Winter.

The Disinvention had begun.

The Purification had begun.

However, although Edmund had taken note of the tapestry and although he had noted its significance, more immediate matters occupied his mind.

As arranged, he and Ulricka were alone.

Edmund stretched his feet toward the fire and leaned back in his chair. He drank from his glass of Spieden Blue. The blue-white liquor warmed his mouth and throat, and it soothed his jangled soul.

He thanked the Gods and the Generations that distillation had survived Eileen's universal cleansing.

Ulricka did not lean back in her chair, nor did she seem to take any pleasure in the fire, neither in its warmth nor in the dance of its flames. She sipped from her glass, but she had no evident reaction to the Spieden Blue.

Was she that jaded...or that ignorant?

Edmund felt he might as well have offered her a cup of Broken Top black tea.

"You wanted to meet," Ulricka said.

"Don't be in such a rush. Find the moment and be *in* it."

"Warrior mysticism?"

Well, what of it? Such aphorisms help to dampen the mind's gyrations.

"Do you remember last year, when it fell to me to be your consort in the ritual copulation?" Edmund asked. "Your hurry to finish the act made me feel as though you found me repulsive. Did you?"

"No," she said.

Her voice had been too level.

"You're not much of a liar. I'm an old man, and you like your lovers young…and female."

She scowled at him. He may as well have been a smear of dog shit on the floor of her audience chamber in the Saraswati Palace. "You weren't my lover."

"I stand corrected. A ritual coupling does not lovers make. Which leads me to an interesting question. You despise Narmer. His ambition frightens and disgusts you. *He* frightens and disgusts you. Why did you take up with him?"

"He's not my lover, and he's not my friend," she said. "I keep him at arm's length and on a short leash."

Edmund believed her, about the leash. Unfortunately, sooner or later, leashes had a way of snapping. "You're taking a colossal risk."

"Politically, I need him to counterbalance you."

"He'll turn on you the instant it serves his purpose."

"You already have."

Edmund was genuinely surprised. "Me? I haven't moved against you. I've no ambition to expand upriver."

"You extracted Royden by force of arms."

"I moved against one of your actions, not against you or your authority or the Cathedral."

She wasn't stupid. She had to understand the distinction. If she didn't the basin was doomed.

"Very well," she said, nodding her acceptance. "But if what you say is true, why form an alliance with Vernon? You hate the man."

The want-to-be pharaoh's plans were the answer. "Narmer—"

"Why convert signal rockets into weapons?" she asked.

"Why kidnap one of my magi? Why send your spies against me?"

"Jinhai worked for Vernon. Was he in your employ as well?"

"No, he wasn't."

The truths behind the facts, the relationships, crackled between them. They swooped and squeaked like questing bats.

Ulricka indulged in a good-sized swallow of Spieden Blue. "How did we end up here?"

It was the sort of question that had no answer.

"The question is, how do we end up somewhere else?" Edmund said, and refilled her glass.

Xenia closed the spy hole.

She could still hear Edmund and Ulricka talking, trying to come to grips with the mess they were making of things, doing their incompetent best to negotiate their way back onto safe ground.

Well, good luck to them!

Xenia was glad she'd convinced her brother to offer Edmund that particular suite, the one on the other side of the wall, and she was overjoyed that the aging buffoon had accepted it.

A private meeting! What a joke! In a warren like this old pile? Those two ought to have known better.

That said, she had no reason to listen further; therefore, she moved away, back into the Hall's hidden recesses.

Around her the tunnel-like passage was pitch dark. It was also dusty, and thick cobwebs filled the corners.

Cobwebs.

Spiders.

She hoped in passing that she didn't step on one, that one of the vile creatures didn't foul itself in her hair.

The floor was cold under Xenia's bare feet, but she hadn't dared to wear shoes. Shoes made noise, and noise might be heard.

Luckily, rats didn't frighten her. They'd left their droppings here and there. She couldn't have expected otherwise, but they had broadcast their turds like seeds, like farmers planting wheat. Perhaps the rats were hoping to bring in a crop of little baby rats, as if they hadn't already overrun the island.

Once her brother's guests had departed—speaking of rats, for the most part—she'd have to send in the ratters. They were terriers, and they positively adored the taste of rodent blood, but not nearly as much as they gloried in the sounds and textures of rodent death.

Looking back on her morsel of spying, she decided that she'd heard nothing new. Well, parts of it had been: the exchange about Jinhai especially.

What had motivated Jinhai?

The chain of cause and effect was far too muddled. She would have to fix that. She and her brother would need perfect clarity if they were to emerge from the months ahead with their clan and their lands intact.

Intact?

She was thinking small.

She was thinking in trivialities.

She was thinking like her poor, spineless brother.

The truth within the truth was that the Gods and the Generations might well have bestowed upon Clan Sauvie an unparalleled opportunity, a once-in-a-century occasion for—Now let's be honest!—conquest!

Conquest.

What a lovely word it was.

Bloody conquest.

The very idea sang.

Bloody conquest. The sort of struggle and triumph that would ring and echo down the centuries, the stuff of monuments, histories, epics, and sagas, the grist of indelible memory.

Eternal and without peer.

If...

If...

One thing was as plain as day: it was time for the Mother Metropolitan to join her sisters among the Gods and the Generations.

A fat brown form with a sharp nose and a long, hairless tail scurried along the passage. Fearlessly, it was heading in the direction from which Xenia had come. It paid her no attention.

Soundlessly, Xenia growled and bared her teeth at it.

Ignoring her, the rat bounded along on its own ratty business.

The diplomatic talks resumed the next morning.

Within an hour, they had entered the familiar channels Edmund had expected, and by midday, they had become deadlocked.

In response to another one of Narmer's fatuous demands that Edmund castrate himself, militarily speaking, Edmund said, "I refuse to withdraw my forces from their current positions. The matter is not open to debate. They are *my* forces, and they are on *my* land."

As the words flew from his mouth, Edmund realized their stupidity, their lack of foresight. What difference did it make where his army was? On his upriver border or back from it.

The whole issue was nonsense.

Worse, it was a distraction from his main purpose. What mattered was delay. What mattered was the appearance of negotiation, not negotiation itself.

He had told himself that dozens of times, had thought it through step by step, had based his plans for this conference on the ironclad necessity to buy time for Vlod, Aerian, and Desmond, to buy time for the rockets.

But then he'd lost his temper and had thrown his preparations overboard. He'd allowed that greasy pig to manipulate him into making a false step.

Very well.

But at this juncture, Edmund couldn't afford to do an about-face. He would have to convince them to persuade him. He would have to be seen to be generously agreeing to one of their requests.

To that end, what he had to do now, over the long run, was to keep Narmer and Ulricka talking, and to do that, Edmund had to accede to their demands, to give ground, step by step, hour by hour, day by day.

The game would be to give in reluctantly, to extract concessions of his own, to say yes through clenched teeth and a happy smile.

Sooner or later, Ulricka had to come to her senses. Sooner or later, she would have to look at a map and realize that she stood between hammer and anvil and that she would have to choose between them or leave the smithy.

Later, much later, after Edmund and Vernon had brought their armies up to full strength, after they had trained them to a fine edge, they could burn the resulting treaties and make good their losses.

SEVEN

Vlod chose to watch the rocket launch from a spot downrange and off to one side. He stood out in the open, unprotected, but with an outstanding view of what was about to happen: clouds of smoke, shooting flames, and flying metal tubes.

He'd made smarter decisions, but needs must.

He had the morning sun behind him. That part was okay. Unless there was a sniper hiding in the trees on the other side of the range.

It was too soon for snipers, though. Spies, yes, but the snipers and the stealthy assassins wouldn't be along until *after* they'd finished their development.

Desmond was a few meters to the rear of the launching tube, off to one side. Out of the way. He had a handy log to drop behind if the test took an unexpected turn.

They'd had several of those—rockets hooking off to one side or the other or, worse yet, reversing course altogether.

It was a large log, though, specially placed for the purpose.

Aerian lit the fuse, ran like a mountain lion with an arrow stuck in his ass, and jumped behind a barricade. It was a three-sided log wall.

They'd tried sheltering in holes and ditches dug in the ground, but the rain and the runoff had turned those into mud pits.

White smoke and orange flame shot out of the lower end of the launching tube.

The rocket streaked from the tube, heading north, toward the far end of the proving ground.

Rather than explode in midair, as so many of them had before, this rocket flew in a high, properly mannered trajectory, like an arrow loosed by an expert archer from a powerful bow.

The rocket flew well.

The propellant burned well.

The rocket climbed well.

It became a mere smudge above the trees, a black stain against the gray sky.

The test was good.

Maybe this time they'd solved the problems.

The rocket was looking good, flying true.

Then, without warning, without the slightest hint, a fraction of a second before the last of the fuel was due to burn out, the motor casing exploded.

It took the explosive charge with it.

The twined explosions made a bright flash and then a gray-black blotch against the sky.

A heartbeat later, the double detonation sounded across the proving ground as a slurred *Kra-Bang!* Chunks and shreds of the rocket body and the casing that had held the charge sprinkled down. They looked like irregularly shaped hailstones.

Vlod, Desmond, and Aerian gathered at the launch site.

Wisps of smoke curled lazily out of the tube, and the sharp odor of burnt gunpowder blanketed the area like a thin, low-lying fog.

After agreeing to the self-evident, that the rocket had yet *again* blown itself to bits before reaching the top of its trajectory, Aerian asked, "The demonstration for Edmund and Wolfram went better than anything we've tried since."

"We've been going for greater range and heaver payloads," Vlod said.

"We need to use thicker material for the combustion chamber," Desmond said.

"Or a different design for the nozzle," Aerian said.

"How about eliminating the nozzle?"

"A heavier rocket body will reduce range," Vlod said.

"We could try another type of gunpowder."

Vlod made a face. "We've been around that barn more times than I can count." He gazed downrange, trying to imagine an approaching army. Infantry, cavalry, archers, lancers, throwing engines, skirmishers rushing hither and thither. Narmer's banners. Ulricka's banners. The minor clans eager to do their bidding, to gobble up the scraps.

"We're nearly out of time," Vlod said.

"A short-range rocket would be better than no rocket," Aerian said.

"We're going down the wrong road," Vlod said.

"Wrong? It's our road," Desmond said.

"We have weeks, not years," Vlod said.

Aerian sighed. It was the sort of sigh a card player sighs when his opponent turns out to have an extra low trump, thus protecting his high, winning trump. While they were fiddling with gunpowder mixtures, fin design, and rocket body walls, Narmer was building transport galleys and forging weapons. "What do you suggest, then?"

"It's time to change directions."

"I don't understand," Desmond said. "Change tactics to *what*? I admit we don't have a useable weapon yet, but we're making progress."

"We don't need to annoy them, we need to kill them."

"Vlod's right," Aerian said. "Whoever *they* turn out to be."

"The uninvited," Desmond commented.

Stomach acid burned up the back of Vlod's throat. Was this how his father had felt when he'd challenged the College of Magi and the Cathedral?

"Exactly," Vlod said, "and what we need is a weapon that will cut them down wholesale."

"We need our rockets to hit their targets," Desmond said.

"No, I'm afraid that won't do," Vlod said.

"Then what will?" Aerian asked.

Vlod's chest tightened to the point of spasm. "We need to teach iron to fly."

EIGHT

The wind gusted across the proving ground, kicking up twigs and rustling the leaves in the trees. It dispelled a measure of the sulfurous odor that seemed to cling to the very ground, to rise from it like vapor rising from the surface of a still pond on a cold day.

"Flying iron? How do we accomplish *that*?" Desmond asked.

"By not skipping steps," Vlod said.

"Care to explain?" Aerian asked.

"Let's tidy up first," Vlod said.

Vlod carried his share of their tools and equipment back into the work tent. Desmond and Aerian followed, their arms loaded with sections of the launching apparatus, broken down to the tube, the lumber, and a bucket of fasteners.

With the pieces and parts in their places, Desmond asked, "Okay, O man of mystery, what steps have we skipped?"

"Unless I'm completely wrong, they're the steps where we teach ourselves how to throw rocks," Aerian said. "Vlod and I looked into it a while ago, but discarded the notion as a distraction."

"I couldn't have said it better myself," Vlod said.

"What are you two talking about?" Desmond demanded.

Vlod said, "Our problems are rooted in our inattention to precedence."

"You're a flowery bastard," Desmond said. "How about you just say what you mean, what ever in hell that is."

Aerian took a sheaf of papers from a hidden compartment in a cupboard, and handed them to Vlod. "Fill him in."

"About what?" Desmond demanded.

"The end of warfare," Aerian said.

"What an optimist you are," Vlod said.

"It helps me to sleep at night."

"I know this girl—"

"Only one?" Aerian said.

"Look, moron, Anna Zehks is a fine girl. She—"

"I'm sure she is."

"I ought to tell you about her," Desmond said. "You'd turn green with envy."

Meanwhile, Vlod leafed through the pages. He was hunting for the sketches of an idea that he and Aerian had worked on for a time. They'd made good progress, too, but, just as Aerian had told Desmond, they'd abandoned the concept. However, they'd done so not because it would have been a distraction. They'd set the concept aside because it would have cost them their very lives.

Vlod found the sheets and glanced over them. He handed the sketches to Desmond, cutting off his enthusiastic description of the incomparable Anna Zehks.

"Forget about rockets," Vlod said. "Here's what we're going to do. We plug one end of the launching tube and layer it with strips of hardwood. We bind the strips in place with iron bands, spaced closely together. Then we use the reinforced tube and a small amount of gunpowder to throw the explosive charge—"

"Or a solid projectile," Aerian said.

"—at the target."

Desmond's jaw dropped. "Have you gone mad? Too many of the wrong mushrooms?"

"Our drawings aren't much better than doodles," Aerian said, "but your imagination can fill in the gaps."

"I hope it doesn't," Desmond said, but his eyes flicked greedily back and forth as he scanned the drawings. He moved quickly from sheet to sheet. "You and Aerian worked on this?"

"For a time. In private. We wanted to include you, but didn't," Aerian said. "My decision. I'm sorry. We set the idea aside because it was too radical."

"Too lethal, you mean," Desmond said. He set the papers on the workbench. He stepped away and pointed at them as though they were a basket of timber rattlers. "*That* is complete insanity."

"Is it?" Vlod asked. "Can you build a rocket that will fly true and explode when it's supposed to?"

"Not yet."

"Maybe never," Vlod said.

Desmond nodded his agreement. It was an admission that they'd been chasing their tails for a dangerously long time. "All right. Maybe never."

Vlod picked up the papers. "Then let's get started on a device that will *work*."

It was past midnight, but dawn was still hours away.

Vernon shifted in bed, not restless, not uncomfortable, but in need of a slight change.

Middle age exacted a price, and this nattering urge to change position was a part of it.

He remembered the midwatch relieving the first watch. (Why the 2000 to 0000 watch, 8 pm to midnight, was called the first watch was one of life's etymological mysteries.) But how long ago that change had happened, he couldn't say.

If he'd been aboard ship, he'd have had the half-hourly bells to go by, but even if he had been, he wouldn't have heard them.

Why not?

Because he had had his attention focused elsewhere.

He and Xenia had sated themselves, enthusiastically and inventively, and by this time, they had settled down. They were relaxed, content to be in each other's company. It was a pleasant emotion, but he could not sleep.

Nor could she.

Xenia lay there and stared at the ceiling.

"Counting the faces in the plaster?" he asked.

"The clouds."

"Why clouds?"

"I like clouds."

She got out of bed and arched her back in a luxurious stretch. She nearly bent the whole way into wheel pose. The posture both flattened and accentuated her breasts.

Was there no end to her flirtations?

No.

She wanted him malleable, obedient, willing and eager to help her, to take her part, to protect her, to obey her, and in exchange she was willing to flatter him, to befriend him, to have sex with him, to ally herself to him, and to one degree or another, to tell him her secrets, her brother's secrets. Value for value.

The image shattered.

Reality, it seemed, was a wrecking ball, a breaker of dreams.

Vernon was an old man, and she was using him, as cynically and as selfishly as her purpose demanded. No holding back.

Two could play that game.

Watching her drop into wheel pose, watching the arch of her body, the fall of her hair to the floor, the subtle curve of her breasts, he promised himself, he swore to himself, that he would put a stop to the fun and games the instant they put his clan in danger. In the meantime, he would use her as much as she was using him.

Promise, promise, promise.

She sat on the window seat and wrapped herself in a blanket. She talked and he listened; he talked and she listened. They traded gossip; they traded information; they exchanged fears.

She poured herself a glass of wine, drank a quarter of it, and shifted from the window seat to the edge of the bed.

"I was wrong about not wanting to be Mother Metropolitan," she said. "The downriver clans need to put Ulricka out of the way, and I'd be as good as substitute as any."

Vernon's eyes snapped fully open. "Ambition, thy name is woman."

"It's not polite to gape."

Vernon schooled his face into a bland expression. "You're suggesting the blackest of the black heresies. Besides, you're not qualified to be Mother Metropolitan."

She waved her hand dismissively. "A technicality. A few beautiful and inspiring rites and I would be. Remember the legend of Thomas Becket?"

"Who?"

"A Christian saint of the Patriarchal Age. You need to catch up on your reading."

He ignored the swipe. Maybe he deserved it for suggesting she wasn't qualified to be the basin's preeminent prelate. "Can you have children?"

She sat bolt upright, shoulders back, head high, neck straight, eyes narrowed. He had deeply offended her. "I'm not barren."

She'd just confessed to two major crimes. First, she had to be using birth control in order to masquerade as barren when she was not, and second, being fertile, she had refused to marry and have children. Either was sufficient to see her burned.

How she'd made it through her year in the Virgins' Pavilion without getting pregnant was anyone's guess.

"How will you explain your sudden ability to become pregnant?" he asked. "They won't elect you if you can't have children."

"Silly boy, I'll bathe in the Pool of Eileen. Don't look so skeptical. Its waters have healed thousands of people."

The Pool of Eileen was on Sauvie's Island and was a major source of revenue for Seldon's clan. Pilgrims were grotesquely willing to part with their money in order to prove their piety or to bathe in its waters in the hope of a miraculous cure, which Vernon mused, amounted to the same thing.

An annual human sacrifice renewed the pool's life-giving powers. Canon law forbade such rituals, but they happened in secret regardless. Every few years the Cathedral made a token effort to stamp them out, but they endured as a mark of religious fervor.

In the pool's case, the priestesses conducted the sacrifices by drowning the victims. Vernon shuddered at the thought. Drowning was a hideous way to die.

Rumor had it that the officiants secretly drugged the victims to the point where they didn't understand what was happening to them.

Vernon scoffed at that idea. The human body seldom let go of life without a fight.

Piety might induce the victims to agree, but instinct would compel them to struggle against their own deaths.

Nor could the victims be comatose. They had to be alive, willing, and aware. To sacrifice a dead, unconscious, or compelled victim was to commit a mortal blasphemy.

Another morbid thought crossed his mind. Rot being what it was, within a matter of days or weeks, the victims would float to the surface of the pool. Attendants would have to be on hand to haul them out. Bloated corpses and decaying body parts were bound to make a bad impression on next year's potential volunteers, let alone on the throngs of pilgrims that visited the pool in the hope of an ecstatic experience.

"Healing waters," Vernon said. "Ought to work. Not many would question it, and your supporters would shout down anyone who dared."

Xenia sipped her wine. "Religions have a way of reinforcing themselves. People will believe anything if there's a tangible advantage in it for them."

"No belief goes unrewarded?"

"If you like."

"You *are* a cynical bitch."

"I like to think so," Xenia said.

Vernon got out of bed and poured himself a glass of whiskey. He sipped it and sat beside her. "I can't picture you as the maternal type."

"I'm not."

"You wouldn't try to pop out a baby every year, would you?"

"Every other year would do."

He nodded. It was a gap of three years between births to a mother metropolitan that set the protopriestesses, the protopriests, the canons, the châtelaines (those with châtellenie, anyway), the mothers superior, and the mothers rector (although not the mothers vicar) to drawing up lists of potential successors. Four years was proof positive that it was time to elect a new mother metropolitan. The onset of menopause was also proof that a new mother metropolitan was necessary. No cycle, no life.

"I hate to think of you dying early," he said.

"Not a chance," she said. "There are outs. Election to be the Holy Mother, for one. Retirement to a hermitage, for another, which the canons *do* allow for under certain circumstances. The have-babies-or-die part of the theology has been under scrutiny for decades, and Ricki herself has stoked those fires recently. Anything's possible."

"What does the metropolitanate buy you?"

"Religious fulfillment. I'm very devout. Didn't you know?"

Late in the afternoon on the fifth day, Ulricka declared the obvious. The talks had stalled. No further progress was possible.

Which was fine with Edmund.

NINE

After they'd assembled the necessary parts, Vlod, Aerian, and Desmond found it uncomfortably straightforward to build the first three prototypes of their new rock-thrower. They didn't dare use its correct name, even among themselves in the dark of night.

A simple series of tests told them how much gunpowder they could use without destroying the tube. A modified version of the same tests established how much gunpowder, with the tube elevated by a given number of degrees, would throw a rock of a given weight how far, plus or minus.

It was a simple function. Diameter of tube, amount of power, amount of angle, and amount of weight yielded distance achieved. It was rather like shooting an arrow from a bow: weight of the arrow, strength of the bow, the angle at which the arrow was loosed.

The results were crude and of limited use, but they were a starting point.

Vlod, Aerian, and Desmond devoted their second week of tests to directed fire. They were not only after range. Now they were after accuracy, too. Could they hit what they were aiming at?

Toward the end of the third day, Vlod carefully studied what they'd accomplished with the afternoon's four shots.

The projectiles had smashed the target into shattered boards and splinters. The target had been a two-meter-by-two-meter square of unpainted lumber held up by cottonwood log posts. It had begun the experiment looking like a short run of a wooden wall. The flying splinters would have cut anyone standing behind the target to ribbons. Any one of the projectiles would have pulverized the poor bastard.

As usual after a test, the air was acrid with the stench of powder smoke. The smoke drifted off to the east, out over Willapa Bay, where it finally and mercifully dissipated.

The cessation of sound after their last shot amplified the silence. The hush was so profound that Vlod could pick out the hiss of the wind in the trees and the rustle of the wavelets on the beach.

"Son of a bitch," Aerian said, his voice an awed whisper.

He'd stretched the words into a muted expression of triumph and horror.

Tears of sorrow and regret ran down Desmond's face.

"It works," Vlod commented.

"We've reinvented the perfect killing machine," Aerian said.

"It didn't take long, not really," Desmond said. "We must have a talent for slaughter."

"The library helped," Vlod said.

Aerian said, "Slaughter? No sane military commander would dare to send men-at-arms against one of these devices!"

"You give military commanders too much credit," Vlod said.

"You've damned us," Desmond said.

"Better us than Clan Iredale," Vlod said.

Edmund went aboard *Koan* and stood off to one side on the quarterdeck, out of the way. Finding such a spot had been no small feat.

The anchor detail raised, fished, and catted the bower.

Under the captain's supervision, the officer of the deck turned the ship's stern to the current and held her in place. The scouts and escorts took up their positions, and the vessels exchanged "Ready!" signals.

At the captain's order, the flags for "Ahead dead slow" were hoisted to *Koan*'s signal yard.

The scouts and escorts responded in kind, repeating the hoist flag for flag, indicating that they understood the order and were standing by.

The captain ordered, "Execute!" and the flags aboard *Koan* were hauled down smartly, transmitting the order.

As one ship, the squadron proceeded downstream at dead slow, clearing their signal yards. Once the ships were clear of Sauvie's Island and its traffic, its shoals and its deadheads, the ships would set their sails and ratchet up their speed.

And a good thing, too. Edmund couldn't return to Fort George soon enough.

When the Great Gate of Shillapoo had fallen politely astern, Edmund left orders that he was not to be disturbed and went below. In the great cabin, he poured himself an impolitely large brandy.

With the drink in one hand and the decanter in the other, he collapsed into the chair behind his trestle table. He had his back to the arc of windows across the ship's stern. The light falling on the table was perfect for reading, for writing. He would do neither. He set down the decanter and made a mental note of the level. He wanted to relax, not get drunk.

When would his muscles unclench?

When would he again feel as though he *hadn't* bathed in pig shit?

He scolded himself for allowing self-pity to overtake him.

He swallowed a boorishly large gulp of brandy.

It warmed his mouth and throat, and the heat spread through his stomach. It was precious little comfort.

A single thought stoked his melancholy: Compared to what he'd just been through—that miserable conference—the bloodiest, nastiest battle he'd ever fought was clean and honorable.

He topped off his glass.

He had asked Ulricka how they might end up somewhere else.

The eventual answer, delivered by the conference, had spoken volumes: The fact was, they couldn't. Their quest to avoid a war had been a fool's errand, played out within a web of naïve hope and inescapable necessity. The forces arrayed against them were blind and pitiless.

Another gulp.

Another flush of warming.

He ought to have brought along a bottle of the good brandy, not the middle-grade rotgut he drank in the field.

On second thought, he ought to have brought a bottle of Spieden Blue.

No, Spieden Blue was more Vernon's line of country than it was Edmund's, in the same way that Xenia was more to Vernon's taste than she was to Edmund's.

She was a treacherous schemer, that one.

Nice tits, but they were like the eyes of a cobra, hypnotic and deadly.

Another analogy came to him.

There were countless joke about praying mantises, weren't there? Yes, indeed there were. Well, Xenia, tits and all, made a praying mantis female look benign.

Poor Vernon.

He'd best count his heads after copulating with that one.

The commands and reports drifted down from the quarterdeck. Their unruffled regularity soothed him more than the brandy did, but they soothed him less than did the prospect of war.

Finally it was upon them.

Finally he could *act*!

He had delayed Ulricka's jihad. He had bought Vlod a morsel of time. Not much, but if Vlod and his people had used it wisely, it might be adequate.

Might.

Might not.

It would have to be.

If not, then Vlod's burning at the stake would illuminate the Inland Empire and the Holy Oregon, and Clan Iredale would drown in a river of blood.

Ten

Vlod held his breath and waited for his chieftain and his chieftain's battlemaster to react.

As the echoes danced from the trees, this way and that across the proving ground, neither Edmund nor Wolfram had jumped for joy. They had not slapped Vlod on the back, nor had they congratulated him on his brilliance.

They weren't that sort of people, and his wasn't that sort of accomplishment.

Aerian stood next to Vlod. Desmond was off on a drunk. Which wasn't as bad as it sounded. Wolfram's people were keeping an eye on him.

The remains of the target stood two hundred meters downrange.

As they had before, the new weapon's projectiles had obliterated it. What remained were shattered uprights, splintered planks, and twisted nails.

"Every time?" Edmund asked.

"Within limits," Vlod said.

The chieftain walked toward the target, and the others fell into step with him.

"Every time?" Edmund asked, repeating his question.

"As far as we can tell, my lord, given the variables," Vlod said. "There's an observable variance between discharges, but as you saw for yourself, it isn't large."

"Less than that with a catapult," Wolfram said.

"Granted, but the throw weight isn't as much," Edmund said.

"It doesn't have to be," Wolfram said. "These projectiles have power behind them."

"That's true," Edmund said.

Wolfram asked, "Why did Desmond go off on a bender?"

"His conscience is troubling him," Vlod said.

"No taste for the stake, eh?" Edmund said.

"He can't decide whether he'd rather be judged by the Gods and the Generations or by Narmer," Aerian said.

"It's not the Gods and the Generations he needs to worry about," Wolfram said. "It's Ricki."

They reached the target. Splinters littered the ground. Most were small, but others were the size of a man's arm. Each had its share of needle-sharp points and knifelike edges.

Edmund picked up one of the medium-size pieces. He crumpled a broken edge. Hunks of fiber fell away. They fluttered onto the ground.

Edmund pointed back up range at the experimental weapon. "How many of those can you build, and how soon can you build them?"

"It's hard to say," Vlod said. "The tubes will be one problem, and adequate supplies of gunpowder will be another. Training the crews. Supplies. Security."

Edmund dropped the piece of wood. "Send me a requisition."

"Yes, my lord."

"We'll need a dozen of them. Eighteen would be better."

"Yes, my lord."

"I want the rockets, too. I want huge, smoke-belching army-smashers. Can you do it?"

"Not immediately, my lord," Vlod said, "but eventually."

"I don't care if they work. All they need to do is belch fire and make noise."

"Yes, my lord."

In a matter of minutes they'd gone from experiment to prototype.

And Edmund had added the rockets back onto the table. Where would it end?

"Focus on the rock-throwers, then. We'll save the rockets for later."

Blessed sanity! "Yes, my lord."

"Can you build eighteen?" Edmund asked.

"Yes, my lord," Vlod said, and felt as though a horse had kicked him in the stomach.

ELEVEN

The door to Ulricka's solarium opened and Narmer strode in, cocky, proud, and overbearing. His clothes were a gauche mélange of Egyptophile ceremonial robes and military uniform. No linen kilt, though. The Gods be praised!

The June day was warm, and Ulricka had expected him to take advantage of it to show off his legs.

Also on the plus side, he had omitted the trumpet volleys, the groveling minions, and the dancing maidens strewing flower petals before him.

As large as it was, the solarium was too small for trumpets. As for the maidens, well, *maidens* were fairly thin on the ground these days. Less than half of the virgins who enrolled in the Virgins' Pavilion for their years arrived *intact*.

Ulricka watched Narmer cross to where she was sitting, hosting an informal but regular gathering of cathedral clergy.

Narmer shoved his way into her conversation with one of the priestesses. "We need to talk," he said.

Ulricka glared up at him. "Make an appointment."

"Now, and alone."

Several heads turned in their direction.

Ulricka wasn't sure whether to indulge him or order her guards to throw him out. A couple of weeks in an antechamber might do him a world of good, and humiliating him in that way would bring her no end of satisfaction.

She ought to have brought him to heel months ago.

"Very well," she said, and motioned to Shabnan, a quick indication that she needed to withdraw for a time.

Ulricka led Narmer into the same adjoining office where she had talked to Vlod.

Ulricka sat down.

Narmer remained standing. He glowered down at her, or glowered as much as he dared.

It was hard, she thought, for someone as unattractive as he was to glower. Glowering required a certain amount of presence, and he had none.

The three and a half weeks since her return to the cathedral had been placid but active. Ulricka's religious and pastoral routines had been a wholesome diversion, a refuge for the poisonous swirl of regional politics. The baby she was carrying had changed from a nondescript presence into a personality.

It spent its afternoons kicking and twisting, and its mornings docile, shifting from time to time. Its nights were a mix that felt as though it was trying to perform calisthenics.

Due to round after round of post-conference, informal, back-channel negotiations, Ulricka had lifted her call for a jihad against Edmund, Vernon, and their allies.

Quite surprisingly, terms had been tacitly agreed.

No more had been said about Dagna's marriage to Gregory, Vernon's son and heir.

Nothing further had been said about Edmund's exclusive control of the Columbia River Bar. Nevertheless, he had reduced his transit and transshipment fees.

He had agreed to withdraw his army from his southeastern frontier as long as Narmer agreed to return to his own lands and stay there.

For her part, Ulricka had redoubled her vow of political and military neutrality.

The parties had backed away from one another. The situation had calmed. It was not unlike an infected wound that has thrown off its infection and begun to heal.

They were not, however, out of danger.

Despite Edmund's rhetoric and assurances to the contrary, his people had not abandoned the development of gunpowder-fired weapons. His magus was making steady progress, but none of his inventions, as far as Ulricka was aware, had risen to the level of being practical.

They were, so far, technological curiosities, not weapons. Even if they were, none had been made public. None had been deployed.

Edmund could abandon the effort at any time.

And he might abandon it, if she could convince Narmer to shut up—Couldn't he please shut up?—about his divine mission to "unify the Two Lands," if she could convince him to go home.

He wasn't going to be the Pharaoh of the Inland Empire and the Holy Oregon, and the sooner he got that through his melon-shaped head the better.

Honestly, how did he live with that grotesque skull? How did he look at himself in the mirror when he shaved or combed his hair?

Ulricka had to admit that for Narmer the past month had been an agony of thwarted ambition. He'd paced the cathedral grounds like a trapped animal. He'd hunted his way through the cathedral's game parks, and he'd copulated and brawled his way through Maryhill's brothels and taverns.

Most telling, he'd left his army camped in the Gorge, a few kilometers above the First Dam. He was blatantly and publically refusing to return to his own lands.

Like a petulant child, he'd dug his heels in and refused to budge.

Had he come downriver to stay?

It appeared so.

"Those two lowland bastards aren't to be trusted," he would reply whenever she suggested he go home.

Now here he was, hulking over her, his face an image of self-righteousness and bottled-up anger.

"It's time to attack," he said.

Ulricka had no need to ask whom.

The pure June light cascaded in through the office windows. It gave

Narmer's face an almost human appearance, apart from the anger in his porcine eyes.

"Attack?" Ulricka asked. "Why? They may as well have capitulated."

Narmer shook his head. "Has Edmund closed down his work on rockets? No, he hasn't. He and Vernon are begging the Goddess to impose another Great Winter."

Spittle had not flown from his mouth, but it had been, Ulricka reckoned, a near thing.

"Go home," Ulricka said. How many times had she already said it? "Give it time."

A knock sounded on the door, and it swung open. Shabnan and a courier entered.

Shabnan and Ulricka exchanged looks. Ulricka had left explicit instructions. Was this emergency genuine or imagined or a convenience?

"What is it?" Ulricka asked.

"Your Beatitude—" the courier began, but stopped short. She glanced from Ulricka to Narmer and back again.

Ulricka said to Narmer, "The view from the terrace is lovely this time of day."

The piggy pink of his face darkened to an honest red. "Since you mention it, Your Beatitude, I have been feeling rather cooped up," he said, and stalked out of the room.

Ulricka noted he'd used the phrase "cooped up". Had he meant to call them a bunch of hens? She wouldn't put it past him, but this was no time for a confrontation over petty name-calling. Besides, he wasn't the only one who was feeling surrounded by hens with nothing better to do than cackle and cluck, scratch and peck.

There were days when Ulricka longed for the company of men. Not the Year King, not the priests, not the sort of men who served in the Cathedral Guard and the various bureaus, but *men*. Genuine warriors. Men who got their hands dirty, men who farmed, ranched, fished, and logged. Mill workers. Sailors. Shipwrights. Bargemen. Blacksmiths, carpenters, and armorers. *Men!* Dirty, ugly, hairy, sweaty, crude, handsome, virile men. Men with pricks a meter long, men who knew what to do with those pricks, and men who weren't afraid to do it.

A disturbing thought assailed her. Could that desire account for her tolerance of Narmer?

No, it could not. At best, he was a paranoid fop dressed up in Pharaonic clothing. Sort of.

Ulricka returned her attention to the messenger. "All right, we're alone. What is it?"

The woman held out a thin sheaf of papers. Two wax-sealed canvas bands held the pages together. The wax showed the seal of the Diplomatic Affairs Committee. "This dispatch arrived from downriver early this morning. Faridah decided you ought to be made aware of it immediately."

Faridah, who chaired the committee, was no alarmist.

"I see," Ulricka said, and accepted the packet.

She snapped the bands and read the first page. It provided an overview of Vlod's work out on the Long Beach Peninsula. As far as Ulricka could tell, his work had produced one illicit triumph after another.

Whatever details the rest of the dispatch contained, the first page alone was enough to impose an end to moderation.

To necessitate a *Jihad*.

Ulricka said, "Please convey my compliments and my appreciation to Faridah."

"Yes, Your Beatitude."

"That will be all."

The messenger left and Shabnan closed the door.

Ulricka handed her the first page, and began reading the second.

The speed with which the runt had advanced astonished her. He had accomplished in weeks an amount of work she had originally estimated would take him years. Was that the way of re-invention: read the archives, adapt the ancient practices to current methods and materials, test, refine, and deploy?

Ulricka read on, page after appalling, dreary page.

The potential for slaughter was unimaginably worse than their defector-in-place had reported when he'd first approached them.

Moderation?

Moderation was a sad hope.

Stability itself was at an end.

Why?

Because the Harmony itself was under siege.

As Ulricka finished each page, she handed it to Shabnan.

When the Crone had finished reading the last of them, she returned them to Ulricka. They comprised a well-arranged stack of death warrants. "The runt and his friends have done it, then."

Ulricka glanced out at the man on the terrace. "It seems our single-minded friend was right."

"No one has ever accused him of being stupid."

"Did he already know when he barged in earlier?"

"He has his spies," Shabnan said.

"They're fast, too," Ulricka said. "Faster than mine. Faridah ought to have brought this to me hours ago."

"Yours produce better information."

Ulricka had her doubts.

She swallowed hard. She was moving too slowly. She was adapting behind the time of need. Her forces were barely adequate to police, let alone to defend, the cathedral and Maryhill, never mind engage a determined enemy.

Deepening her sense of dread, if she could believe the unbelievable, Vlod had washed the last grains of sand out from beneath her feet.

Ulricka gestured with the pages. "Lies?"

"A measure of exaggeration, surely, but we expected them to achieve as much, or nearly as much."

Ulricka hadn't. She'd expected them to crawl back into their holes and fish, and hunt, and dredge, and pilot, and farm, and go on cattle raids.

She had *not* expected them to prepare for a general war.

She said, "I'll have to give Narmer what he wants."

"Is that wise?"

"Do I have a choice?"

Shabnan's brow wrinkled. "I doubt it."

"About our defector," Ulricka said. "Pull him out. He's of greater value to us here, and of no value to us if he's dead."

At the end of yet another staff meeting, Edmund asked, "Whatever became of Desmond?"

"Gone. Slipped away in the night," Wolfram said. "My people have checked his haunts and hideouts. He's not on Iredale land."

"Off on a drunk?"

"Too soon to tell," Wolfram said. "We'll find him."

TWELVE

other Metropolitan Ulricka paced her terrace. No, she corrected herself, she waddled her terrace, back and forth, round and round.

Apart from bringing Desmond upriver to Maryhill, apart from the couriers shuttling back and forth, and apart from readying the Cathedral Guard to take the field, June had been a quiet month, on the whole. There'd been no disasters, no crises. Narmer's fits of temper had created amusement rather than disruption.

And now it was July, the month named for Julius Caesar, that ancient and bloody conqueror. He was as much a legend as he was a man. July: good weather and dry roads; the very month for war. None better. Caesar's month!

From the moment she'd announced her intention to deploy with the Cathedral Guard, the Saraswati Palace had been in a quiet state of uproar. People scurried to pack the things they imagined she and her household might need.

As the draymen carted the boxes, trunks, and bags down to the warehouses by the docks, their wagons choked the streets of Maryhill.

This was the morning of Ulricka's scheduled departure downriver. The sun was already high, and the day was growing more oppressive by the minute. Only the awnings and the breeze made the morning tolerable.

How she had once enjoyed the dry heat of this stretch of the river!

Once.

Today she felt like a dripping blob of fat, supported on two pillars of fat. She was draped in gauzy cloth that had turned sticky the instant she dropped it over her shoulders.

How did men-at-arms stand it, girded about as they were with leather and metal?

Would this pregnancy never end? She wanted the *thing* out of her. She wanted it *away* from her. She wanted it *gone*!

She didn't care where they took it or what they did with it as long as she never had to deal with it again.

Self-loathing obliterated her inner, private tantrum.

It was the loom of war. It was the prospect of wholesale death, of those piles of corpses, and of the pits they'd be shoved into.

How noble! How compassionate! How fraudulent!

It was the pain in her back and the agony in her bladder.

It was the nausea.

During her other pregnancies the upset had faded after the first few weeks, but this time it had held on, tormenting her.

It was the fat, and the clumsiness, and the ups and downs of her emotions, and the ooze and trickle of her oily sweat.

It was the fear of her own death. A breach. Worse. Tearing. Bleeding. Infection. Death. Quick or lingering; painful or an unconscious slipping away. However it came, death was death.

A sandal rasped on a paving stone.

Shabnan.

An unexpected panic, malignant and spreading, threatened to unbalance Ulricka. If she and Narmer did not win this war, the victors, Edmund and Vernon, would rip her baby from her womb and dash its head against the nearest rock! They would raze the cathedral and slaughter those sheltering within its precincts. They would topple the henge and burn the libraries. They would hack down the grove and desecrate the sacred graves. Holiness would be at an end. The Harmony would die.

Her pace faltered.

Her feet would not obey her will.

"They're ready for you," Shabnan said.

She couldn't catch her breath, and her legs felt as though they had detached themselves from her body.

Ulricka sat on a granite bench. She had not so much sat as she had collapsed. She had collapsed rather than faint from cowardice.

Shabnan approached and looked down at her.

Ulricka looked up into the older woman's face, into her eyes.

The crone's strength came from her will, and it informed her features.

Her strength had not rendered her hard. It had not tainted her from within. Rather, it had made her beautiful and compassionate.

"You're safe, Ricki," Shabnan said. She sounded as though she were a brilliant sunrise dispelling a dark night. "The cathedral will endure. You *shall* prevail."

Ulricka believed her, not out of wishful thinking or ignorant hope, but because whatever Shabnan said carried an indelible stamp of truth.

War or no war, win or lose, Ulricka's baby would be safe and cared for. No harm would come to it.

The baby kicked against the front of her belly.

A morning kick. No sleeping in today. An excited, happy kick.

Kick, kick, kick. The life inside her was gathering itself to enter the wider world.

Ulricka chuckled at that thought.

Once her baby had entered that wider world, it was sure to wish it hadn't.

———

From the edge of the firing range, Vlod watched Brenna's approach.

She was on horseback. The size of the horse made her look small and fragile. She wasn't hurrying, but she wasn't dawdling, either. She had dressed in her marine field uniform—an ordered pattern of browns, greens, and blacks—rather than in whatever clothing had come to hand. Her cloak was an old, dark-gray monstrosity she'd worn for years. She'd belted on her best battle sword. It was a true murderer, light, sharp, supple, resilient. She had a battle knife on the hip opposite and dirks in her boots.

She wasn't in full kit but near enough.

There was trouble afoot and no mistake.

Brenna reined in and slipped off her horse. She said happily, "Ulricka's cutting stakes and gathering firewood."

"No pitch?"

"It's on its way."

"What's happened?"

A canvas-wrapped box was tied behind her saddle. She pulled it down and handed it to Vlod. "I was asked to give this to you."

"By whom?"

"A grateful admirer."

The box contained two bottles of Van Horn Butte Reserve whiskey. A note in Gluth's hand said, "You've made a lot of drunks very happy. Stay alive."

Vlod grinned so broadly that the muscles over his cheekbones ached.

"Booze?" Brenna asked, a touch of puzzlement in her voice.

"I did a favor for a friend."

"Must have been one hell of a favor. Van Horn's a close second to Spieden Blue."

"You didn't ride all the way out here to play delivery boy. What's happened?"

The laughter vanished from her face. "Their armies have arrived at Seldon's."

No wonder she'd dressed in uniform.

Narmer's commanders had moved fast. The ancients said that armies moved on their stomachs, but Wolfram insisted that they marched on their hands and knees. Fifteen kilometers a day was about average. Narmer's forces had done considerably better. Transport by barge would explain it. They must have taken to the river.

Narmer and Ulricka, the leaders themselves, together with their suites, had arrived at Seldon's four days ago, within an hour or two of Edmund and Vernon's departure. Their last-ditch attempt to sway Seldon to their cause had ended in failure.

"Has anyone else joined his pharaonic majesty?"

"Phelan hasn't, but at least a dozen lickspittles have. Jean-Pierre among them."

"Firman?"

"He remains my father's trusted ally."

Firman's lands were inland, to the south and east of Iredale lands.

"I'm surprised he hasn't found an excuse to join her."

"He may," Brenna said.

"Balance of forces?" he asked.

"Four to one. Their favor."

"Shit! How soon before they attack?"

"More than a week but less than two. They'll have to work themselves into a passion, first. Wait to see who else might stumble out of the trees."

"Every spear helps."

"Not if you've done your job, magus."

THIRTEEN

From the observation tower on the bluff above Morven's Gate, Edmund surveyed the positions on the bottomland below. His telescope, which had been his grandfather's, brought the figures and features into clear view. He matched what he saw to what his staff had marked on the map in front of him.

An army's position at the very outset was critical, especially when the ratios were against it. He and Vernon were outnumbered, but they had the superior *position*. Edmund held the high ground, and he owned the approaches to it.

Narmer had drawn up his forces on the flat beyond Morven's Gate. He had packed them tight into what amounted to a box canyon. He was relying on numbers and a narrow front, and because he was, because of his stupidity, hundreds would die to no good purpose.

With Vlod's new weapons figured into the mix, an Iredale-Innes-Martin victory was as assured as anything in battle could be.

However, despite these assurances, a spasm of doubt, of fear, gnawed at Edmund. He felt as though a worm had burrowed into his gut.

He'd felt something similar only twice before. The second time had been when the Third Battle of Slaughters Dike had spiraled out of control and he'd had to retreat from the riverbank, to flee from the same flat of land that swept in an arc below him now. He'd taken his army right up the bluff, right past the spot where his observation tower now stood.

Morven's Gate hadn't existed then, and Vernon's army had choked the bottom end of the road. They had thronged the slope wherever they could find purchase enough to climb. Only Wolfram's near-suicidal rearguard action had prevented an outright rout and wholesale slaughter.

It had been that near disaster that had convinced Edmund to build the wall. It fronted the riverbank, and then ran inland. It bisected the bottomland. The wall's strongpoint was Morven's Gate.

The Gate was only stone, timber, and bronze, but it shone in the sun. Morven had shone in the sun, too, tall and proud and unafraid.

Like so many of that sort, Morven had been reckless. It had been that recklessness, that heedless daring, that had resulted in his death...on an insignificant cattle raid, on a lark.

The first time Edmund had felt the worm had been the night at the Cathedral Henge of Eileen the Immortal, a few short days before Her Beatitude, the Most Blessed Thora, Mother Metropolitan of the Inland Empire and the Holy Oregon had come downriver and had burned Vlod's father at the stake.

Thora and her lackeys had outmaneuvered Edmund, both religiously and politically, and he had found himself debarred from countering her monomania, her hatred for Shivananda, for Vlod's father.

She would have cautioned or disciplined another man, but she and powerful factions within the College of Magi had been determined to snuff out Shivananda and to silence and block anyone and everyone who had or who might come to his aid. It had been political thuggery at its most ruthless, at its most effective.

Their threat to Edmund's clan had bludgeoned him into silence. Their power had stayed his hand.

Thus, with nothing to do, with no way to prevent it, Edmund had watched an innocent man, a righteous man, burn.

Vlod had shown greater courage that afternoon than any child of nine ought to have had to show. He'd kept his grief in check until it had been safe for him to let it out.

Edmund had long since sworn himself to the child's protection, but watching the flames and the child's self-control, he had repeated his oath a thousand times over.

Now, thanks to the paranoia of an upriver madman, Edmund had put Vlod himself in danger of following his father onto the stake.

Nor was Vlod the only one he'd endangered. Aerian. Royden. Wolfram. Himself, come to that.

For them, for all of them, it was win or burn.

Only Desmond was safe, and for no better reason than that he had gone over to the enemy—the selfsame enemy now arrayed across the bottom land below, at the foot of the bluff, carpeting the ground like the ash from a forest fire.

Edmund closed his telescope. "Their banners are pretty."

"Hmm," Vernon said, and lowered his own telescope. "The streamers are a nice touch, especially on the lances."

"A nice touch on a parade ground," Wolfram said.

"Hmm." Vernon pointed his telescope at a position near the river but toward the rear of Narmer's lines. "Seldon's down there. I hadn't expected him to show himself so blatantly."

"Any army of Seldon's is a poor thing," Wolfram said. "Too much silk and not enough practice."

"Don't underestimate him," Edmund said.

"What do your augurs say?" Vernon asked. "Mine are shitting their pants."

"I thought I detected a septic tang on the wind," Wolfram said.

"Mine aren't much better," Edmund said. "One says we'll win. The other says the Gods and the Generations refuse to speak."

"Typical," Vernon said. "What does Vlod say?"

"That the Gods and the Generations have left it up to us."

"*Not* typical," Vernon said.

"But very *Vlod*, if you take my meaning," Wolfram said.

"He's worth ten thousand of anybody else," Edmund said.

"You're overestimating him, surely," Vernon said.

"Under," Wolfram said.

"Then Ulricka will want him dead," Vernon said.

"As did Thora before her," Wolfram said.

Edmund reopened his telescope and rechecked Narmer's forces. Xenia was there. She was in modified battledress and had ridden out in front of her brother's position. "What's Xenia up to?"

"She must have deployed with her brother," Vernon said.

"Why would she have deployed?" Edmund asked. "She's no warrior."

"She's much worse: she's a cunning politician," Vernon said.

Edmund went over to the ladder and stepped onto the top rung. "I'm going down at the Gate."

Dagna rode out onto the edge of the bluff at the same time that her father and uncle, far below on the bottomland, rode into the timber-and-stone fortress that was Morven's Gate.

Dagna and her companions reined in off to one side of the road. A jumble of action surrounded them. The majority of units followed the road on down the slope, but others hesitated, waiting for stragglers and orders, while still others dug in along the edge of the drop. Elsewhere, a group of engineers were assembling a line of six trebuchets, an unbelievable number. They'd placed the massive throwing engines to cover each of the enemy's potential lines of approach up the bluff, should the worst happen and the Gate or the wall fail to hold against Narmer's attack.

The day was obese with the odors of men and horses, of wood and steel, of fodder and leather, of cooking and latrines, and of the leftover mud from a summer rain, mingled with horse urine and dung.

They were familiar orders, but they were inexplicably and oddly changed out here in the open, out here in the midst of a gathering army, an army that was arraying itself for battle, her father's army.

And because she was her father's daughter, Dagna also caught the intoxicating amalgam of anticipation and reluctance, of fear and excitement. She could almost taste it in her mouth. *Battle!* Today, tomorrow. The day after at the latest.

The end of talk.

The beginning of action.

The settlement of old scores.

The harbinger of a new balance.

She was not supposed to be here. She had been forbidden. With just cause. From a certain point of view. She was Edmund's only fertile child, and because she was, her father and her uncle had deemed her too valuable to risk in battle. Therefore, they had left her locked her away in Fort George.

Dagna had made another choice. It was their fault that she had come. They ought to have used real locks.

Dagna's escape from safety had been surprisingly thrilling. She had waited until the chaotic urgency of the fleet's departure had calmed into the hurry of the rearmost units to cast off. Then she had changed into field uniform, assembled a group of adventurous friends, and had headed east, on horseback, upriver toward Morven's Gate.

She had done so not because she was defiant, pigheaded, or blind to the danger, but because she was an officer in her father's army, her clan's army. She was a commissioned lieutenant in, and the honorary colonel of, the 23rd, a rapid-deployment infantry regiment.

The 23rd were, she liked to think, light cavalry on foot. They were fast, mobile, and deadly. She was proud of them, and she would not shame herself—or them—by not joining them in the field. She wasn't stupid enough to imagine she could command them anywhere but on a parade ground, but their commander would, she was certain, allow her to stand with them. She could wield a sword or an axe in the line, and she could stand in a shield wall with the best of them.

Better still, she might prove to be the 23rd's only on-hand archer. She could pick off the enemy with the same skill she used to kill deer, elk, and bears. Her war bow rode in its saddle scabbard, her quiver next to it.

A lieutenant trotted over toward Dagna. His name was Vexler—a good hand with logistics but useless in a fight.

"Welcome to the party," Vexler said.

"Thank you."

"I hear you weren't invited."

"I didn't want to miss the fun."

"Good for you. We'll have plenty to go around."

"Let's hope so," she said. "Where's my regiment?"

"They're down on the flat: middle right, between the third and fourth towers."

She picked out the 23rd's blue-and-white standard.

"How soon can my friends and I join them?"

The lieutenant's expression darkened.

Dagna had no trouble reading him.

It had just dawned on him that she was deadly serious. She hadn't come out on a lark, to see and be seen, but to fight in the battle.

The lieutenant looked flustered and embarrassed. His emotions retreated into annoyance. Her presence was one more unwanted problem in a day that was a morass of unwanted problems and critical trivialities.

"You don't belong here," he said.

"My regiment is here."

A voice off to her right said, "He's right. You don't belong here. You belong down there, with your regiment."

The man who'd spoken was dressed in the cavalry uniform of Vernon's army. He was tall, broad through the shoulders, and narrow through the hips. He had dark hair, dark eyes, and a square-jawed face, strong rather than imbecilic. He was Gregory, Vernon's son and heir, the man her father wanted her to marry.

"Are you making fun of me?" Dagna asked.

"Why would I do that?"

"Lieutenant Vexler is in charge of this post."

"He is," Gregory said.

She cocked an eyebrow. Did Gregory imagine that she was the pampered lady of a pampered court?

"I couldn't do my job without him," Gregory said. "I've been given command of the road and Vexler reports to me."

Command of the road? Why would they have given him command of the road? He ought to have been down at the wall.

"May we pass or not?" she asked.

With a nod of his head, he beckoned her off to one side.

Curious about what they couldn't say in front of Vexler and her companions, she followed.

Reflexively, her left hand dropped to the pommel of her sword. She hadn't brought her katana—which was far too splendid a weapon to use on Narmer's thugs—but her workaday infantry sword.

"I can tell what you're wondering," he said. "Why in hell am *I* up here? Well, I'm up here for the same reason that you were told to stay back there." He pointed to the northwest, in the direction of Fort George. "My father despises my brother—"

Who didn't? Bevan, Gregory's younger brother, was an eminently despisable rodent of a man.

"—and if I'm killed, he'll inherit."

With a hint of fellow-feeling, she said, "Then I guess we're in the same boat." She pointed toward the space between the third and fourth towers. "My regiment is down there."

"Very well," he said, relenting. "But promise me you won't try to prove what a hairy-chested warrior you are."

She glared at him. "I'm not a complete idiot."

"You do have a reputation."

Yes, she supposed she did, but at least she hadn't meekly allowed her father to humiliate her. It would be a cold day in hell when the 23rd went into battle, a real battle, without her.

That Gregory couldn't say as much, painted him with contempt.

"You have me confused with my sister," Dagna said. "Brenna's the gut-'em-and-stack-'em one in the family."

"What about Wolfram?"

"He doesn't bother with stacking. Leave 'em to the ravens and gulls. That's his motto."

Gregory laughed. It was a remarkably pleasant sound. It tumbled across the top of the bluff and cascaded into the valley below.

Dagna and her group joined the flow of personnel, wagons, and pack animals on the road.

"What did Gregory say to you?" Mirakin asked. She was a dark, stout woman, large boned and plain-witted. She was what people saw: an uncomplicated junior officer, assigned to Dagna's personal guard, a good but occasional companion.

"He told me to stay alive."

"Good advice." In a brighter tone, she asked, "Will you marry him?"

"That's what we're here to find out," Dagna said. "I'll never love him."

"Why's that?"

Dagna didn't want to answer. She said, "I wonder if Father will attack over the open ground or defend the wall."

"Your father? He'll attack."

Fourteen

The officers' mess in Morven's Gate was a rough-hewn room in the base of the keep-like structure that abutted the riverward gate tower, itself a massive, no-nonsense fortification. The room's walls had been constructed of double-stacked logs. The double-stacking was rather like the wall of a traditional log cabin but with an extra, staggered run of logs. The overhead consisted of open-beamed timbers with steel reinforcing plates, and the floors were of thick, sawn planks, planed, but neither sanded nor finished. The fireplace had been made with a mixture of basalt and river rock, whatever, it seemed, had come to hand.

Edmund's allied chieftains had crowded into the room. Either they sat on the benches or tables, or they stood or leaned around the perimeter.

Oiled leather and oiled weapons, human sweat, horse sweat, and horse-shit-laced mud tinged the atmosphere.

One of the minor chieftains was bug-eyed drunk. Conceivably, he was seeing double.

Vlod took in the theatrics, for that was what they were, the absolute extent of what they could be. Edmund, Vernon, and the others had come too far to turn back.

"You're making us into criminals and heretics!"

The speaker, who was railing at Edmund, was Thorian. He wasn't the double-seeing drunk, but he was one of the dozen or so minor chieftains who'd rallied to Edmund's banner. Thorian was the chieftain of Clan Limnehah. He and Edmund had had their differences over the years, but in this case, Thorian had brought along several of the other minors. Where he led, they were likely to follow. "For the love of heaven, smash the damn things."

Thorian added, "I mean it: burn the wood and melt down the iron. Pretend they never existed."

Railing at Edmund: never a wise move.

Thorian continued his addendum, "If you don't destroy them, we will!"

A round of assent blistered through the room.

Threats were an even worse move.

Loyalty, or professed loyalty, bought only so much forbearance.

Vlod expected Edmund to respond, but Thorian wasn't finished.

"That magus of yours—" Thorian pointed at Vlod "—will have the whole basin down on us."

Wolfram asked, "Would you prefer to haul Narmer's barges at his rates, pay for his grain at his prices, erect his obelisks, pay his taxes, and build his pyramids?"

"Two can play that game," Thorian said.

The man was a hopeless idiot, Vlod thought.

Because Edmund was the Iredale's chieftain, he was expected to be fairly magnanimous when confronted. That same expectation did not extend to Wolfram, the clan's battlemaster. Happily, Wolfram could act in ways that Edmund could not.

Thorian was saying, "Do you want to be banned from every henge in the basin? Do you want your name excluded from the *Dirge*? Do you want to wander in the Wilderness of Limbo for eternity?"

Limbo, Vlod mused, was far from accepted theology. Doctrine stated that those whose names were not recorded in the Dirge suffered annihilation. They did not enter into a sort of transcendent anteroom. They couldn't. They did not exist.

Restoring a person's name to the Dirge restored the person to existence, restored the person to presence, to the consciousness, to the memory, of the Gods and the Generations. It was as though that person had never not existed.

The mechanism by which this miracle was accomplished was endlessly debated, but in the end, it was a mystery, incomprehensible. It merely *was*.

Thorian rushed on to answer his own questions.

Would he never cease?

How he loved the sound of his own voce, the glow of his own self-righteousness.

Thorian was saying, "I don't want to suffer eternal death. I want to live with the Gods and the Generations forever. I want the Goddess to bless me and mine."

"Ulricka's favor is no guarantee that the Goddess will smile on you," Wolfram said.

It was as close as Vlod had ever heard the battlemaster come to making a serious theological statement.

Lambrock spoke up. "The Harmony *is* in turmoil," he said. He was the drunk, and his words were slurred and overloud. His remaining teeth were the color of fried bacon fat. "Can't you feel it? The Harmony is in pain." He stared around the room. "Our clear duty is to heal it."

Another round of assent bounced off the walls.

"The ground will swallow us if we don't," another one of the minor chieftains cried. He was in a state of acute panic. In a different situation, his exclamation might have had a comic overtone, but not here, not now. Here and now it sounded like betrayal.

The pack of them sounded like superstitious old men.

Earlier in the day, Vlod had arrived at the top of the bluff, having traveled overland, with ten freight wagons. They had contained barrels of gunpowder, crates of projectiles, and a dozen of the new weapons, together with the small, modified wagons, disassembled for transport, that would serve as their carriages.

He'd managed to cobble together an even dozen of death-belchers, not the eighteen Edmund had wanted. They were not works of art.

Vlod had also brought the crews to man the weapons and the workmen to repair them in case of need. With five men-at-arms for each of the weapons, one captain and three lieutenants to keep the whole unit in order, and two workmen to make emergency repairs, he had a total of sixty-six people. They'd been scrounged from other units and from last-minute volunteers. Many were well beyond service age.

Their training, including Vlod's, had been scant at best, a herky-jerky, fits-and-starts series of improvised sessions in which they learned—or figured out—the barest rudiments of how to train, elevate, sponge, load, and fire the weapons. The bulk of what they'd learned had been gleaned from Vlod and Aerian's developmental work.

In effect, their techniques were made up out of whole cloth or had been broadly adapted from archery. None of it was based on real-world experience in battle.

And yet, the experience was there, waiting to be adapted to the new conditions.

Vlod notice one of the old men. He had a quiet optimism about him, a natural competence that saw him through when training or precedence were of little or no use. The handle of his battle knife flashed whenever a ray of sunlight hit it. It was an exceptional knife. It had a snarling lion's head on the pommel and intricate scrollwork on the guard. Both were now well-worn with the hard use than only a lifetime of fighting and peace could have put to them.

Vlod had left Aerian at Fort George to guard their work sites—and their notes and drawings!—from curious eyes and grasping hands. He had also been tasked with the construction, outfitting, and delivery of as many more of the new weapons as possible.

Wolfram met Vlod at the top of the road.

Peering into the back of one of the freight wagons, Wolfram asked, "Can we position the weapons up in the battlements?"

"Not without rigging a crane," Vlod said.

"They won't be of much help, then, unless the bastards break through."

"Why not deploy them outside the wall? Intersperse them in the line?" Shield walls, cannon walls. It made a kind of sense.

A crowd of onlookers gawked and pointed at the ungainly weapons, which were more or less stacked like fireplace logs in the backs of the wagons.

"How easy are they to move?" Wolfram asked. "Are they mobile?"

"Not without better carriages."

"Fixed positions, then."

"In effect. A degree of mobility, but nothing to count on in a hurry."

Wolfram made a face. "Better than nothing."

"Yes, my lord."

Wolfram's expression softened. "You've worked a miracle, little magus! You truly have. Aerian, too."

"Thank you, my lord," Vlod said, but he felt ashamed of the pride he felt, his pleasure in Wolfram's approval.

If Vlod and Aerian had worked such a miracle, then why had Aerian begged Edmund not to use the weapons, and why was Vlod so certain, down in his bones, that he'd opened a path to the very pit of hell?

Miracle or not, burning was too good for him.

Word spread, and by the time Vlod's wagons arrived at Morven's Gate, several of the allied chieftains had gathered to gawk at them and to complain.

They demanded to see the new weapons for themselves, and they demanded explanations. When Vlod told them what he could about the weapons, which wasn't much, they howled in alarm.

Why hadn't Edmund consulted them?

Who'd given Vlod permission to devise such abominations?

How would Ulricka react?

No doubt she was already cutting stakes and gathering firewood!

This was no time for jests. How was she going to react? She'd have to counter is some manner. She couldn't possibly let such demonic weapons go unanswered. She was sure to suppress them, ban them, purge them, them and anyone who had anything to do with them!

All of which to Vlod seemed like an odd set of questions and fears. He would have thought they were beyond caring how Ulricka reacted, how she might respond.

She'd made her position clear. She had drawn her sword. She had mounted her white horse. She had launched a crusade. She had embarked upon a jihad. She was out for their blood.

Edmund had arrived and had taken the confrontation into the officers' mess.

Now, as the chieftains' second- and third-tier subordinates crowded in, not wanting to miss the show, and as the temperature in the room climbed, Thorian jabbed his finger at Vlod. "You had no right!"

Thorian's stupidity, his preening in the spotlight, was making him careless as well as stupid.

Did such men never learn?

Vlod answered his own question. No, they never did.

Breaking his silence, Vlod said, "You sound like a frightened cottager. How many of us are supposed to die in order for you to preserve your illusion of divine favor? Those weapons will save lives—ours *and* theirs."

"You conceited little fool!"

In the pit of his psyche, the last coffer of Vlod's self-control wavered. Keeping his voice bland, just as Master Yokashima had taught him to, he said, "I suppose you can always crawl back to your manor and teach yourself to grovel like an Egyptian peasant."

Thorian yelled incoherently and lunged at Vlod.

Edmund's magus sidestepped, and Thorian crashed into a knot of chieftains and retainers. He whirled around, but rather than resume his attack on Vlod, he faced Edmund.

"This is your last chance," Thorian said. "Will you or will you not put a stop to that insolent whelp?"

"You will never again raise a hand to one of my people," Edmund said.

Thorian's face was the color of blood, and his breath was coming in quick, shallow gasps, his chest heaving. "Will you stop him or not?"

Wolfram's hand dropped to the handle of his battle knife.

Edmund said, "My brother Thorian, you have no authority within Clan Iredale."

"Then you leave me no choice," Thorian said. "I must go to the mother metropolitan."

"To beg her forgiveness?" Edmund asked.

Edmund's voice was steady, but his hands were flexed with rage. This, too, Vlod had seen before.

Thorian said, "To beg her to call a halt to your insanity!"

Again the man's logic was impeccably flawed. Why else had Ulricka come downstream with Narmer, if not to force the Iredales back into a posture of unwavering obedience?

Thorian turned his back on Edmund and started toward the door.

In a seamless succession of moves, Edmund drew his battle knife, grasped Thorian under the chin, pulled his head back, and slit his throat.

The move was deep, quick, and powerful.

It had been so much so, that Vlod had heard the sharp rasp of the blade as it had passed across one of Thorian's cervical vertebrae.

Blood sprayed from Thorian's neck, like water shooting up from a ruptured main.

Vlod drew his sword and moved into a position from which he could defend Edmund or attack into the chieftains and their subordinates at will.

Other swords flashed out.

Wolfram drew his sword and his battle knife, and moved to protect his brother.

Edmund pushed Thorian away.

No one attacked.

Clutching his throat, Thorian stumbled and collapsed onto his knees.

It was the best place for him.

He tried to scream but produced only a wet hiss. He pitched forward, sprawling onto the floor, and convulsed as his life drained away in a red froth.

The room resounded with alarm and protest, but no one else drew. The drawn swords remain unraised, and the undrawn weapons remained sheathed.

Edmund had called their bluff.

Edmund had made the example, and the example had driven home the sobering truth of the business they were about. Live as free men and women, or grovel as Narmer's slaves.

Graedfoye, Thorian's battlemaster, slowly sheathed his sword.

Other swords and knives slid back into their scabbards.

Wolfram's and Vlod's were the very last.

To Graedfoye, Edmund said, "Remove your dead."

"Yes, my lord," Graedfoye said.

Graedfoye and two of his men dragged the corpse from the room.

It left an instructive smear of blood.

That evening, Vlod checked the sentries guarding the new weapons. He chatted with the members of the crews, the workmen, and the lieutenants, and, with that done, he spoke to their captain in private.

The captain was four or five years younger than Vlod, but he had risen through the ranks fast. He did what needed to be done, without the need of a superior telling him to do it. At the same time, he had a knack for never presuming, for never getting out ahead of his superiors. He never whined, and he never lost his head. He was too good to be true, but there he was.

They walked toward the base of the wall.

For one reason or another, Vlod was keenly aware that on the other side of that timber-and-rubble wall, at a distance, were the enemy forma-tions. Only the sentries atop the walls and the patrols farther out stood between them and Narmer's massed forces.

Of the captain, Vlod asked, "Settled in over here?"

"Snug as we ought to be."

"Water? Food?"

"Enough of both. Water barrels filled and ready."

"Good."

Vlod's flow of questions stalled. He had drawn near the nub of his concern, but he had no idea of how to ask it. Vlod wanted to break through his own restraint, but in the end, he said, "Make sure the crews get a good night's sleep. The same goes for you."

"Yes, sir," the captain said.

"Thank you, Captain," Vlod said, and rounded back toward his tent.

———

When the captain strolled into the circle of firelight, one of his lieutenants asked, "What did the magus want?"

The captain wasn't about to tell them that Edmund's magus wanted to be reassured, that he was scared out of his wits. The captain was bedrock certain that what was troubling Vlod wasn't the battle itself. He'd heard too much and seen too much of him in a fight to believe him a coward. It was the new weapons, the untried crews, the not-quite-spher-ical shot, the so-so gunpowder.

Vlod, Aerian, and their people had thrown the whole it together in a manic rush. Only the Gods and the Generations knew whether the weapons would work or blow themselves apart, whether the crews would follow the evolutions as they'd been trained or lose their heads and run amok. Would they remember to sponge out the barrels between discharges or would they shove gunpowder down onto a leftover piece of smoldering wad? It had happened.

But the captain had anticipated his lieutenant's question and had his response ready. With a lecherous grin, he said, "He doesn't want any of you to go off chasing after whores tonight."

———————

Neither awake nor asleep, Vlod listened to the three o'clock watch reports. When they'd finished, he tried to sleep, but he couldn't. He tried to meditate, but he couldn't.

After the four o'clock reports had cascaded from post to post, Vlod tried to perform various katas, but he found it impossible to enter into the flow of any of them.

When reveille sounded at five, he dressed in field clothes.

He formed up with his crews and received the captain's muster report. Vlod could hear other units repeating the ritual throughout the encampment, between the wall and the bluff.

Rather than babble at the crews about duty, glory, and honor, he dismissed them to breakfast with orders to hitch up the teams the moment they'd finished. Then he went to find Wolfram.

The clan's battlemaster had his ways, and one of them was to adjust his plans at the last minute.

Vlod had drawn to within twenty paces of Wolfram's tent when a commotion broke out farther along the wall, down toward the corner where it swung northward and ran along the edge of the water. Four burly men-at-arms were carrying a loaded litter in through one of the secondary portals. Once cleared, they headed up toward the gatehouse.

Vlod thought to ignore the excitement, but then he saw the runners. They darted back and forth between the litter and the tents, between the portal and the gatehouse.

Vlod crossed the yard and fell into step with the litter.

A blanket covered a corpse.

"Who is he?" Vlod asked.

"Thorian's battlemaster," one of the bearers said.

The muscles at the base of Vlod's spine tightened.

He lifted the blanket.

Deep gashes covered Graedfoye's face. He looked as though an animal had clawed it. But that wasn't right. None of the cuts were parallel.

Graedfoye's eyelids and eyes were gone. Fish, or gulls, had reduced the sockets to bloody gouges. Graedfoye's lips, which had been on the fleshy side, had been ripped off. Gulls, then.

"What happened?" Vlod asked.

One of the bearers said, "They found him down on the beach."

"Any idea what killed him?" Vlod asked. He hoped that a specific question would yield a specific answer.

The leader of the four called a halt and they set down the litter. He rolled the body up onto its side and turned the head. He pressed the chin down toward the chest. "See for yourself."

Just at the hairline, at the nape of the neck, but off to one side, was a small wound. It was about a centimeter wide.

"Stiletto between the vertebrae," the leader said. "Give it a quick twist —" he snapped his imaginary blade through a short arc "—and no more spinal cord." The gleam in his eyes marked him as an amateur killer, the sort who was called out now and then but who spent most of his time limbing felled trees or pushing a plow or gutting fish. "The poor bastard never knew what happened." The grin again. "Well, maybe for an instant he did."

"Thank you," Vlod said, and stood away from the body.

"No trouble," the leader said, and the party resumed its progress toward the gatehouse.

Vlod angled back across toward Wolfram's pavilion.

Graedfoye's murder had been an assassination. Whoever had ordered it had intended it as a warning. Within minutes, the whole camp would understand.

They would understand that they had been warned, but would they understand the warning? Were they to be loyal to Edmund and Vernon, or were they to switch sides and be loyal to Narmer and Ulricka?

Figuratively speaking, a warning rocket had been sent aloft, the requisite attention had been garnered, but the signal flags had yet to be hoisted.

The Limnehahs would be teetering on the precipice of open revolt. Their chieftain and their battlemaster both struck down within less than twenty-four hours. Thorian's case was plain: open defiance openly punished. Graedfoye's case was different. He had been killed in secret. The rank and file were bound to suspect treachery.

Vlod had expected runners and commanders to have thronged the area outside Wolfram's tent. Instead, he found only a couple of sentries and a single runner.

Inside, Wolfram was hosting Edmund, Vernon, and the spy Ziellottes. They sat haphazardly around a table, as though each had taken the chair nearest to him when they'd sat down. They were halfway through breakfast, and the tent was heady with bacon, coffee, eggs, and fried potatoes. The bacon's aroma made Vlod aware of how hungry he was. He hadn't eaten much of anything the day before, and this morning he'd had coffee and nothing else.

Which was beside the point.

Why was Ziellottes here?

Vlod shook off the question. Edmund and Wolfram, no less than he, would do whatever they had to do, while Vernon, naturally, would act in his own best interest.

"Come and sit," Wolfram said. "I asked them to send extra. You haven't eaten, have you?"

"No, I haven't," Vlod said.

He sat down and entered into the flow of breakfast. Their conversation never rose above the level of chit-chat and never touched on Thorian.

At the end of the meal, the table fell into an expectant silence.

Ziellottes took the hint and stood. "Thank you for breakfast, my lord," he said.

"The pleasure was mine," Edmund said.

Ziellottes bowed and took his leave.

Edmund refilled Vlod's coffee mug.

"Thank you," Vlod said.

It was not unlike Edmund to serve his subordinates. He never took it so far as to make himself subservient and, indeed, it often worked to emphasize his power.

Vlod sipped his coffee and waited for the axe to fall.

It wasn't long in coming.

"Are the new weapons ready for deployment?" Edmund asked.

"Yes, my lord," Vlod said. "Say the word and I'll have them set up outside the wall."

"How long will it take?" Vernon asked.

"An hour or two at the most," Vlod said. "We won't be digging them in."

He wasn't comfortable talking about the new weapons in front of Vernon, but he didn't have any choice. Vernon was an ally, at least for the moment. Which was all that could be said for any ally.

"As fast as that?" Vernon asked.

"Yes, my lord."

The operation would require a minimum of further effort. By now, the crews had hitched the horses to the carriages. They would need an hour or so to drive them out through the gate, position, secure, and load them.

Sighting them in?

Well, during the night Vlod had realized that if Narmer's army charged in a mass or if his archers grouped themselves in a block, then aiming the new weapons wouldn't involve much.

Vlod and his crews had tables of powder charge, throw weight, elevation, and range expected to be achieved.

The field was already scored with stone range markers. Years ago, the gate's first military commander had set them out. Their purpose was to allow the crews of the gate's throwing engines to zero in quickly and easily, and it was to this purpose that Vlod intended to put them now.

With any luck, he'd be able to drop projectiles to within a few meters of any stationary target and to punch them right into an advancing formation.

And then the fun would begin...

Edmund kicked up an eyebrow at him. "Breakfast didn't agree with you?"

Vlod realized that he was grimacing. Scrambling for an excuse, he said, "Too much coffee."

"Second thoughts?" Edmund asked.

Leave it to the Iredale chieftain!

Vlod swallowed hard and decided to take the risk. "One or two."

"Tell us?"

"Yes, my lord." The ritual allowed Vlod to voice his opinion without appearing to complain. No doubt, Edmund would have used whatever pretext he could find in order to ask his question. The time for recalculation, for second and third thoughts, was before he'd committed to the battle. Vlod said, "Once we use these weapons, we'll have no way to *un*use them."

"No, I wouldn't think there would be," Vernon said. "It's not like resheathing a sword, is it?"

"What's your point, Vlod?" Edmund asked.

"I agree with Aerian, my lord," Vlod said. "We ought to demonstrate these weapons before we use them against Narmer's army."

Edmund's expression didn't change, but the quality beneath it hardened. "I've gone around that barn with him. He's an idealist. I'm not." Edmund sipped his coffee. "Never mind that he brought it to me behind your back."

"It's a good idea, nevertheless."

"I agree," Vernon said. "No matter how vile it is, any weapon that can be used, will be used, and the niceties be damned."

"I agree with Vlod," Wolfram said. "A demonstration might be a good idea."

"Good ideas have a way of killing people," Edmund said, closing the discussion.

"Yes, my lord."

To Wolfram, Edmund said, "Show Vlod where we've decided to place him."

Wolfram unrolled a map of Morven's Gate and its immediate surroundings. He traced a line a few meters away from the wall on the river-side of the main gate. "Narmer's heaviest concentration is toward the water," he said. "With the new weapons there, near the gate, we'll be able to use them to maximum effect."

They'd planned a forward defense, then: aggression and protection in one throw. They'd concluded that it would be better to destroy Narmer in the field than allow him to abandon a siege and escape with his army intact. Their objective was not defense against an invasion, but the annihilation of a would-be conqueror.

Which left Ulricka in an odd situation. Did Edmund intend to annihilate her, too?

Vlod could see the justice in it, but the proposition left him with a sense of dread.

"Comments?" Edmund asked.

"The ground's good there," Vlod said. "We can fire at an angle across the field, out toward the river if they take that option, and, of course, straight into their advancing units."

At this juncture, questions about ultimate objectives and the mother metropolitan's fate were beside the point. Edmund had assigned Vlod to a position from which he could wreak the maximum amount of slaughter possible. As the enemy approached, Vlod's crews could steadily decrease the elevation of their weapons until they were firing pointblank.

Aerian was right, or at least Vlod hoped he was. No one, not even a delusional cretin like Narmer, would order his men-at-arms into such a slaughterhouse, and if he did, they might well refuse to go.

In the back of Vlod's mind, however, a warning was sniggling about the suppurating egos of men-at-arms. As often as not, the martial understandings of duty and honor overrode the human will to remain alive.

A runner rushed in. "My lord," she said, "Narmer and the mother metropolitan have ridden onto the field. They're deploying their forces."

The runner was very young. Her face was flushed, and her eyes shone with excitement.

With a studied nonchalance, Edmund rose to his feet. "Very well." To Wolfram and Vlod, he said, "The day is upon us." To the runner, he said, "Pass the word for the commands to deploy their people along the wall and to make all necessary preparations."

"Yes, my lord."

"Here's the important part: no one is to set foot outside the gate until I give the command. Understood?"

"Yes, my lord."

"Very well, then. Off you go. Keep your head down and don't volunteer."

"Yes, my lord." Smiling from ear to ear, the girl sprinted off.

"I'd best see to my people," Vernon said, and strode out of the tent.

To Wolfram and Vlod, Edmund said, "Shall we see what the *father* metropolitan and his lapdog bitch have for us?"

FIFTEEN

Vlod followed Edmund and Wolfram out of Edmund's tent.

Details and units were hurrying in every conceivable direction, and men-at-arms were racing to the battlements.

Had they left it too long?

Shouldn't they have been in their places at sunrise?

No, it was better to leave such histrionics to the enemy.

Signals were flashing between the top of the bluff and the gate, and from tower to tower. Runners were racing back and forth like mosquitoes on a summer evening in a bog.

They climbed to the battlements.

Brenna hurried up, scanned the field. "They've concentrated toward the river."

"As expected," Edmund commented.

"It seems the pharaoh is out to turn our left flank," Wolfram said.

"We don't have a left flank to turn, not yet," Edmund said. "He's shadow boxing."

"Could be," Wolfram said. "What about an attack, then? Is he attacking?"

"The wall? I don't think so."

"It's a trifle weak over there."

"Where are his siege towers?" Edmund asked.

"Good question. Where are they?" Wolfram asked, speculating. "If he means to attack the wall, where in hell are they? Why hasn't he brought them forward?"

The purpose-driven chaos around them was ratcheting up. Units rushing to their stations. Bugles blaring. Sergeants shouting themselves hoarse. Corporals bullying and chivying with the self-importance of future dictators.

The smell of crushed grass and broken sod filled the air, together with those of cooking fires newly doused.

"Could he be making his parry and riposte *before* we've thrust?" Wolfram asked.

"Is he that smart?" Brenna responded.

"He thinks he is," Edmund said. "It seems the ground isn't unreadable, after all." To Vlod, he said, "Deploy your weapons. He'll advance right onto them. Go out *with* the infantry, not ahead, not behind."

"Yes, my lord," Vlod said, and left the battlement. He took the stairs down to the ground so rapidly it felt to him as though he either negotiated them in one jump or than he had flown down, stooping like a bird of prey.

He was a third of the way across the yard when he saw Ziellottes. The spy was ambling toward one of the stairwells leading up to the battlements.

Against all reason and duty, Vlod followed him.

They were near the top by the time Vlod caught up.

"Hello," Ziellottes said. "I expect you want to talk."

"I do," Vlod said.

Hurrying men-at-arms buffeted past them.

Vlod and Ziellottes continued up to the battlements and found a place out of the immediate crush. It was a crude, three-sided storage shed. Ziellottes sat down on a water cask.

Vlod asked, "Did you kill Graedfoye?"

Ziellottes sighed, his disappointment plain. "Why bother yourself about Graedfoye?"

"His death was unnecessary."

"You're a fine one to decry unnecessary death."

"Answer the question," Vlod said.

"He would have rallied his people to Ulricka's cause. Others would have followed. Inevitably, he would have taken up where Thorian was— shall we say?—cut off."

"Did you do it?"

Ziellottes' face was better than any mask. "I can't say." He reached into his cloak and produced a folded dispatch. The seal was broken. "Graedfoye was down on the beach. There was a terrible accident." He pointed at the dispatch. "I took that off his body."

"You searched the body because...?"

"Narmer's courier hasn't washed up yet. Read the dispatch."

Vlod unfolded the paper. It contained a crude version of Edmund's order of battle: unit names, strengths, possible dispositions, who was in favor and who was out.

Vlod's arms and legs went cold. If the dispatch had gotten through, Narmer would have had an insurmountable advantage.

"Why haven't you given this to Edmund?" Vlod demanded.

"An opportune time has not presented itself," Ziellottes said.

By which he meant that he was reluctant to convict himself of murder. Moreover, what difference would the information make to Edmund's preparations? None. They would amount to little more than an annoying distraction.

Truly it was said that the bulk of a spy's work consisted in remaining silent, in choosing the moment.

"You can give it to him whenever you think best."

"When would that be?"

"When he's alone."

Vlod wasn't stupid but this was one of those times when acting stupid might be the best move. "I don't understand," Vlod said. "Thorian and Graedfoye are dead."

Ziellottes smiled one of those knowing smiles that he let slip from time to time. "Their spirits stalk the land."

"Are you saying that Clan Limnehah is likely to bolt?" Vlod asked. "Doesn't that only increase the message's importance?"

"I can't tell you whether they'll switch sides or not. Edmund's success, if he succeeds, will hold them. No one runs away from victory."

"That's true," Vlod said, but he could think of countless cases in which field commanders had done just that, buckled when they ought to have attacked, shown mercy when they ought to have lopped heads. Still… the saying held true.

"I can, however, tell you this much," Ziellottes said, "Edmund expects you to hammer Narmer's army into a bloody pulp. No games. No qualms. No mercy. I suggest that for your own sake, and for his, that you do no less." He smiled pleasantly. "Murder the bastards."

Sixteen

Edmund and Vernon's combined forces poured out through Morven's Gate and the wall's secondary portals. They created a many-channeled flow of men, horses, and arms. The order of battle included infantry, cavalry, archers, pike men, and crews to work the array of mobile throwing engines—catapults, ballistae, and mounted crossbows—that the units brought along with them.

As Vlod and his officers readied the new weapons and their crews, Vlod worried that Edmund had taken a terrible risk. If the battle turned against him, it might be impossible for the army either to retreat back through the portals or to flee from in front of the wall. They might end up pinned against it.

If the Limnehahs switched sides and if others followed their example, the Iredales and the Innes-Martins would face annihilation.

The niceties be damned! Vlod had no choice but to deliver Graedfoye's intercepted dispatch. It wasn't immediately critical—the Limnehahs may or may not be planning such vile treachery—but the positioning and installation of the new weapons was. The course of the battle could easily depend on them. Come to that, so could enforcing the loyalty of the Limnehahs. The jelly-spined weren't likely to desert the winning side.

For the moment, then, Vlod had no way to complete the task Ziellottes had entrusted to him—to murder as much of Narmer's army as possible—without delivering the intercepted message.

Why the crafty old spy would pass along the job to Vlod was a question for another time.

The minutes raced along.

Narmer's forces formed up, but they did not advance, nor did they dig in.

Edmund and Vernon's forces deployed. They did not advance, nor did they dig in.

The flow of men-at-arms and weapons into the lines continued.

The last of the new weapons went into its place.

As intended, the weapons remained mounted on their low, stripped-down wagons, on their carriages. The crews set out barrels of water and tethered the draft horses a reasonable distance away. Powder kegs and neat stacks of wadding and shot sat close at hand.

With their preparations complete, Vlod and his unit had nothing to do but wait for the battle to begin.

It was time to play at being a spy.

Vlod turned the unit over to its captain, borrowed the man's horse, and galloped back through the Gate.

He found Edmund pacing along the battlements, on the inland side of the Gate. He had Wolfram, several unit commanders, the commodore of the squadron charged with holding the river, and the commander of Morven's Gate with him.

Time was running out. Like it or not, the situation would have to do. Perhaps this was why Ziellottes had given Vlod the dispatch, because only Vlod had the ghost of a chance of separating Edmund from the people around him.

They fell silent as Vlod approached.

"You ought to be with your weapons," Edmund said. His voice was hard.

"It's urgent, my lord," Vlod said.

"What is?"

"A private matter, my lord. I'd delay bothering you with it if I could, but I can't."

"It can't wait?"

"No, my lord."

Edmund stared at him, but then sighed. "Very well." Turning to the group, he said, "We'll need a moment."

The group moved farther along the wall.

When Edmund and Vlod were alone, Edmund said, "You said it was urgent."

"It is, my lord," Vlod said, and handed Edmund the dispatch. "I believe that Ziellottes intended to give you this at breakfast."

"Then why didn't he?"

"He said that the time wasn't opportune."

"He's too cautious by half," Edmund said. "What is it?"

"A dispatch that Graedfoye was attempting to pass to one of Narmer's couriers."

"And the courier?" Edmund asked.

"Dead."

"Thorough fellow, Ziellottes."

Edmund unfolded the paper, scanned it, refolded it, and slipped it into an inside pocket.

"Ziellottes making trouble?" Edmund asked.

"I shouldn't think so, my lord."

"Very well," Edmund said. "Return to your unit."

"Yes, my lord."

"Keep your eyes open, little magus."

"Yes, my lord. Always."

———

Earlier that morning, long before sunrise, Edmund had reinforced his skirmishers on the flat.

Now, with the day racing toward its purpose, they made no effort to hide their presence. On the contrary, they were positioned to act as a shield behind which the army could draw up in good order, free from harassment.

As Vlod rejoined his unit, he was glad the skirmishers were out there, on the ground between the armies.

"Welcome back," the younger of the two lieutenants said.

"You didn't think I'd abandoned you, did you?" Vlod asked, making a joke.

The lieutenant chuckled. "No, but you might have been shanghaied into another outfit."

"Now, now, shanghaiing is strictly illegal. Everyone says so."

"Including the poor bastards who come from too far off the coast to swim...or so their captains imagine."

More chuckles, a few nods from experience.

Suddenly a rider galloped out through the Gate. He rode out onto the flat between the armies and spurred his horse from concentration to concentration of skirmishers.

Each time, an officer or a sergeant directed him farther along.

Eventually, he reined in, dismounted, and talked to one of the men-at-arms, an officer.

Vlod watched the scene.

Gradually, with a dull pang, he realized that the officer the rider was talking to was Dagna. She had slipped through her father's fingers and had joined her unit.

Edmund, or Wolfram, must have sent the rider, poor man, to fetch her.

Vlod chuckled to himself at the temerity of anyone, Edmund included, who dared to try to persuade Dagna to accept safety when her unit was in danger.

The rider pointed emphatically toward the gate. The skirmishers and Dagna made gestures of their own, and, sure enough, after a final gesture toward the gate, the rider remounted his horse and rode back toward the wall. He entered through the gate.

Meanwhile, Dagna paced back and forth.

Vlod suppressed a laugh. Whatever else Dagna was, broodmare or not, she was a warrior—as far as her fertility would allow.

As for Brenna, there was no shred of compromise. She was a warrior through and through.

The captain of Vlod's unit said, "We'll be at it soon enough."

"No, we won't," Vlod said. "We have hours yet."

"Hours?"

"Hours. They have one last round of demands and refusals to wade through. It'll be noon and then some. Unless they spring a surprise."

Edmund, Vlod thought, could well be right in his decision to accept battle here and now. This could be his and Vernon's last best chance to have done with Narmer. If they delayed, there was a good chance the would-be Pharaoh of the Upper and Lower Columbia River—the Two Lands, as he phrased it—would gain unassailable strength. The current odds of four to one were bad enough.

Edmund could be right about the weapons, too. Maybe their power would come as a shock, and maybe that shock would turn the struggle. If they demonstrated the weapons, as Aerian had suggested, that shock would be irrevocably lost. They would have alerted Narmer.

But what about the shock to Edmund's forces? How would they respond to the use of the new weapons? To the thundering detonations and to the wholesale slaughter? Would they tolerate it, or would they switch allegiances, as the Limnehahs had nearly done? Would shock and outrage outweigh the will to survive as free people?

On the far side of the flat, the standards of Narmer's armies, including the Cathedral Guard, fluttered like a colored line of breakers against the green of vegetation and the blue of sky and the white of clouds beyond them.

The sun had driven the lingering chill from the morning, and the harsh summer light made the colors brighter, as if the trees, the sky, the ground, the river, and the people were illuminated from within.

Crows, a stunning black, filled the green-topped trees, white-and-gray gulls, their beaks a vibrant yellow, swooped and fought over discarded scraps of food, and high in the vault, an eagle soared, his head gleaming white. He circled above the field. Waiting. His cry was shrill, and it echoed like a trumpet volley from the bluff behind Morven's Gate.

Seventeen

Ziellottes listened to the eagle's cry. It was distant and slightly muffled. It was an arresting sound, especially on a clear summer day, drifting, as it was, into the Mother Metropolitan's pavilion.

The echoes thinned. Disappeared. And Ziellottes accepted a cup of tea from Ulricka's serving girl, a Child of the Cathedral, perhaps twelve, a henge brat, through and through. Stamped for life.

It was unlikely that Ulricka had poisoned the tea, but it was also unlikely that it would be anywhere near drinkable. Ulricka's household had no appreciation of tea. They took a hideous delight in their vile herbal concoctions, but strong, black tea escaped them entirely.

Ulricka's pregnancy, the physical discomfort of it, had carved gullies around her eyes and mouth. Once upon a time, Ziellottes thought, she had experienced her pregnancies as mystical events that united her with the Great Goddess. Once upon a time, they had confirmed her status as the Goddess's avatar.

Year by year, things had changed. These days, as was so plainly written in her face and on her body, she experienced her pregnancies as nine months of unremitting nausea, exhaustion, and alternating hormonal floods and droughts that hurled her back and forth between elation and depression, between desperation and panic. In between these states, Ziellottes joked within the privacy of his own mind, reigned either panicked desperation or desperate panic.

For how many more years would she be able to endure it?

For how many more years would she put up with it, exchanging agony upon agony for an existence she had come to despise?

Failure did that.

Fear did that.

A remembered joy, never to be recaptured, did that.

There were too many people who thought of the Goddess as the universal loving mother, as the one who comforts and nurtures.

Only novices and morbid idealists refused to see the Goddess's other aspect. The Goddess was closer to Kali, the Black Goddess, than they had any stomach to acknowledge or any willingness to embrace. She was war as well as peace, miscarriage as well as birth, death as well as life, destruction as well as creation.

Creation destroys; destruction creates.

Kali Puja.

Ziellottes sipped the tea. It was black tea, not the usual steeped hedge clippings. It was a good sign. It was hot, which was a better one. Its aroma betrayed too much honey, though, and a surfeit of cinnamon.

Ulricka and her household had taken no small amount of trouble with the tea. As well they might. What was at stake in this conversation was of immeasurable importance.

Perhaps it was, after all, a day for extravagant tea.

For these and for other reasons, common politeness among them, Ziellottes smiled his appreciation, and the serving girl withdrew.

Ulricka asked, "What are Edmund's demands?"

Ziellottes sipped the tea. He was authentically surprised. It wasn't as bad as he'd anticipated. Quite good in fact. Excellent when he considered it. Cinnamon. Not too much, but enough to add flamboyance. How nice!

"I don't understand the question, Your Beatitude," Ziellottes said. "He isn't about to allow you onto his lands."

"We'll swat him like a gnat," Narmer said.

Narmer. He was like a pustule on the face of an otherwise beautiful day.

Ziellottes kept his expression neutral, his personal feelings sequestered.

"Edmund is no gnat." To Ulricka, he said, "To avoid this battle, you must return upriver, approve the marriage between Dagna and Gregory, and renounce any claims to the river bar. I assure—"

"None of which is going to happen," Narmer said, intruding where he didn't belong. "I have five men in the field for every one of his!"

"As much as five to one?" Ziellottes asked. His own figures put the number closer to three-and-half to one by the time the noncombatant personnel were accounted for. Edmund despised baggage trains. Narmer couldn't move without them.

Narmer squared his shoulders and puffed up his chest. "I could claim six."

Ziellottes smiled to himself. Narmer had blundered! "*You* have six to Edmund's one? You *alone*?"

Ulricka cocked an eyebrow.

Ziellottes had scored. She would not allow Narmer to marginalize her. She had used her moral and religious authority, her prestige, to put their combined armies in the field. They had gone to war under her standard, not Narmer's.

"A role in the management of the river mouth is ours by right!" Narmer said.

His demand sounded like the squeak of a petulant field mouse, disappointed by the diminutive size of the piece of cheese he'd found next to a garbage can.

For Ulricka's benefit, Ziellottes said, "He dredges the channel; he maintains the aids to navigation; he provides the bar pilots."

As though he hadn't heard a word, Narmer continued, "Edmund has squeezed a fortune out—"

"Which he has spent maintaining the bar and its approaches," Ziellottes said.

"He's a greedy upstart who—"

"I *am* sorry to interrupt you, my lord, but could you assist me?" Ziellottes said. "I must leave soon. Tell me, is the tide fair or foul for a trip upriver by boat?"

Narmer's face went blank. "I can't tell you. Why would you expect me to be able to? I have people for such menial work."

Ulricka didn't bother to hide her smile. "Edmund could tell him," she said, "and he could tell him whether it was a spring or a neap."

Thank you, Your Beatitude! Aptly put.

Could the upriver cretin tell the difference between spring and neap? Flood and ebb? High and low?

Narmer made a disgusted sound and threw himself back in his chair. Its front legs lifted off the floor, and he had to throw himself forward to keep from falling over backward.

"Our dispute isn't only about the river," Narmer said. "Edmund has defied the will of the basin for far too long."

"He's defied *your will* for far too long, you mean," Ziellottes said.

"Are you taking his part?"

"I'm taking no one's part," Ziellottes said. Graedfoye and that unfortunate courier might beg to disagree, had they been able to do so. "I am curious, though. Whom does your ambition benefit?"

Narmer's face blanched. "I don't have to put up with your insults!"

"Yes, you do," Ulricka said.

"What? Why do I?"

"He's my guest," Ulricka said.

Narmer gritted his teeth.

Regardless of the day's outcome, Ziellottes would have to watch his back with obsessive care for the next several months. Not that he didn't watch it compulsively as a matter of routine, not that it wasn't an ingrained reflex.

Nevertheless, Narmer was not the sort of bullyboy to allow a search for the truth to go unpunished.

Narmer was, Ziellottes observed to himself, a lot like Thora, the previous mother metropolitan, in that regard.

Ulricka asked Ziellottes, "Let's have it. Will Edmund turn over the runt or not?"

Dagna watched the rider emerge from the main gate and gallop across the open space between the armies. The rider was headed in their direction.

"It's another one of my father's errand boys," Dagna said.

Mirakin asked. "Who'd he send this time?"

As the rider closed the distance, his cavalry uniform gave him away.

"No, I was wrong," Dagna said. "It's Gregory, Vernon's son."

Mirakin spat on the ground.

Moments later, Gregory rode up and dismounted.

"Hi-ho," he said. "Having fun?"

"What's the password?" Mirakin demanded.

"Bullheaded stupidity," Gregory said.

"Advance to be recognized," Mirakin said, and made an elaborate bow.

"What are you doing out here?" Dagna asked.

"I hope to die gloriously in battle."

"Fat chance," Dagna said. She nodded off toward the lines of banners on the far side of the field. "If they advance, we'll fall back."

"In theory," Gregory said.

"In practice, too. We're a pack of confirmed cowards."

He made a sweeping gesture with his right arm. "The truth is, I'd like to take you away from all this."

"What about me?" Mirakin asked.

"You?" Gregory asked, teasing her. "Sorry, but you're chopped liver."

"Oh, shit," Mirakin said, "and here I was hoping..."

"I'm staying put," Dagna said.

"Then so am I," Gregory said.

Was he serious? He couldn't be.

"I don't need you to protect me."

"Pretend," Gregory said.

Shading her eyes, Mirakin looked past Dagna and Gregory, toward Narmer's lines. "Rider coming."

Vlod had barely finished a routine scan of Narmer's lines when a horse and rider emerged from them and galloped toward Morven's Gate. The rider wore hunting clothes. Body, arms, legs, neck, and head—every part of him had the short, stocky shape of a water barrel. A gray ponytail hung toward his shoulders.

Ziellottes.

He was leaning low over his horse's neck.

The captain pointed at him. "That's that the spy, isn't it? The one everybody's talking about?"

"No one else."

"What do you think he's up to?"

"He's delivering Ulricka's final ultimatum," Vlod said. He glanced at the sky, at the sun's position. "I was wrong about the time."

"When the tide turns, it turns with a vengeance."

Narmer and Ulricka's forces dressed their lines and brought their throwing engines forward.

Vlod's mind scattered in a multitude of directions at once. Not to be left out, his stomach felt as though it had folded over on itself.

Time crawled.

Ziellottes reached a point that was about a third of the way into open space between the massed armies.

Time slowed further.

Riding hard, Ziellottes crossed the midpoint, and seconds later, as though time had decided to race forward, he was in among Edmund's forward skirmishers. They waved to him as he galloped past. Clods of dirt flew from his horse's hooves.

A staggering numbness engulfed Vlod. He tried to ball his hands into fists, but his fingers refused to close. His vision shrank to a gray blur surrounded by a black tunnel.

Although unable to explain why, Vlod realized that his love for Edmund and Clan Iredale left him with no choice but to gamble everything on his ability to kill cattle in as gruesome a manner as possible. He had to make the worst of slaughterhouses look like a summer's outing.

He called the captain closer.

Shock worked both ways. The new weapons would shock the enemy, but they would shock Edmund's and Vernon's armies, too. The likelihood that the Limnehahs and others would witness butchery, rediscover their allegiance to the Mother Metropolitan, and desert in her favor had tipped the scales.

Tipped.

It was the last bit of added weight.

Already in one of the pans was the duty to avoid as much death as possible. Aerian might have the right of it, but whether he did or not, the obligation to make an honest attempt was undeniable. The chieftains and the Mother Metropolitan had to see for themselves firsthand what they were facing, what they were about to unleash, *before* they committed their armies.

"Sir?" the captain asked.

Vlod's chest ached as though a saddle cinch had been tightened around it.

"I want—" The words stumbled. He tried again. "I want you to—" Again they collapsed. Vlod ran his tongue around the inside of his mouth. "I want you send one of the lieutenants back into the complex, requisition two steers, and bring them here as soon as possible. No delays. None."

<hr>

From the top of the gate tower, Edmund watched Ziellottes approach the gate. He could have only one possible destination and only one possible purpose. Edmund sent a runner to ensure that the sentries admitted the spy.

While Edmund waited for Ziellottes to arrive, he studied the field. Narmer's disposition was meticulously correct. The manuals and treatises couldn't have specified better, nor could they have offered any improvement. But the battle's first clash would collapse those elegantly squared ranks and files.

Wolfram stood next to Edmund. Vernon and Trevor were off to one side. A dozen officers and runners, plus a half dozen minor chieftains had also crowded onto the observation deck.

Edmund opened his telescope. Ulricka's forces weren't an army, not as such. Her army was the Cathedral Guard. It was six smallish units. Horse and foot. No artillery.

Which raised the question, what were they doing in the line?

Narmer ought to have held them in reserve or used them as tactical reinforcements, messengers, skirmishers, and the like. People to fill gaps.

Had Ulricka's field commanders gone mad? Or had they given up thinking for themselves?

He moved on.

Next to Ulricka's forces were Seldon's people, a proper army. Brother and sister were with them. Xenia wasn't in battledress, apart from a highly polished, intricately worked cuirass, but neither was she dressed for a summer picnic.

Her plan would be to withdraw when Narmer, or Ulricka, gave the signal to advance. Perhaps she'd tend the wounded or carry water.

Be that as it may, for the moment, she was in the line, a demonstration of her martial ardor. Since the Mother Metropolitan was making a show of going to war, then it was incumbent upon Xenia to do likewise. After all, she wasn't even pregnant.

Edmund said, "Xenia's over there. Close to the Sauvie's standard."

Vernon had his telescope to his eye. Doubtless, he'd already spotted her.

"I see her," Vernon said. "She's next to her brother."

Edmund wondered how Ulricka would respond to Seldon's support if she learned that Xenia had her eyes on the metropolitanate. Had Vernon told a tale out of school or had Xenia intended him to let her ambitions be known?

Xenia wouldn't have told him if she hadn't wanted him to pass the word on down the line. Was Vernon a party to her plans? In one way or another, he had to be. But to what end? He couldn't be fool enough not to realize she was using him, nor could he be besotted enough with her to allow it.

Was he stupid enough to think that if she were the Mother Metropolitan that he would be able to manipulate her?

No, arrogance has it limits.

Boots drummed on the stairs. The sound pulled Edmund's attention back to the immediate. What news, he wondered, had Ziellottes brought? What news and what demands?

The lieutenant was on his way, sprinting and dodging through the crush by the main gate.

To the captain, Vlod said, "I'm going to need someone with a level head. Thanks for volunteering."

The captain had done no such thing, but he grinned and said, "My pleasure, sir. What's afoot?"

"Hitch a team to the last weapon in line, the river end, and stand by to act as driver."

Ignoring the others on the platform, Ziellottes approached Edmund. "Good morning again, my lord. Do you have a moment to spare?"

Edmund closed his telescope. "A moment, yes."

Ziellottes said, "May we talk in private, my lord?"

"We are in private," Edmund said.

It was the only thing he could say. In this situation, on the cusp of battle, anything else would have been an insult to his subordinates and allies.

"Very good, my lord. The Mother Metropolitan will withdraw in exchange for Vlod. She intends to try him for heresy."

"Like father, like son," Wolfram said.

"What has he done?" Edmund asked. "What heresy has he committed?"

"His new weapons violate the Harmony."

Wolfram said, "I approved them."

"Indeed, you did, but she'll settle for him." Ziellottes continued to Edmund, "She also wants your promise to destroy the new weapons you have and any designs that Vlod and his team may have drawn up, including their notes and so on."

"What is his pharaonic majesty promising?" Edmund asked.

"He undertakes never to attempt to build such weapons. Ulricka promises to ensure his compliance."

"With what?" Wolfram asked.

"Her good graces and the threat of eternal damnation," Ziellottes said.

"He doesn't believe in eternal damnation," Wolfram said. "He believes he will ride across the sky with the sun, or like the sun, or as the sun." He made a self-deprecating face. "I've never been too clear on that part."

"You have the gist near enough," Ziellottes said.

One of the minor chieftains said, "It would give us time to build up our strength. What's the life of—"

Vernon glared the imbecile into silence.

No one spoke.

But the man was right, Edmund thought. What was one life against the lives of hundreds today and the prospect of an overwhelming victory at some point in the future?

The question itself was disgusting and repulsive. It was no better than the loathsome bleat of a whining coward. To answer in the affirmative was to lie down in the nearest gutter. It was to enlist one's self as worse than a slave. It was to become non-human.

Avatar or not, Ulricka was out of her depth.

Breaking the silence, Edmund said, "Vlod is my affair."

"Yes, my lord, he is, but heresy is hers," Ziellottes said.

"Every time she doesn't get her own way, she screams heresy."

"She *is* the avatar."

"She's *one* of how many?"

"Dozens, but she's the one you have to deal with at the moment," Ziellottes said. "Your lands fall within the province she governs."

"I could relocate them," Edmund said, and made his decision. "Tell Her Beatitude that we await her pleasure. If she and Narmer want a war, they have nothing more to do than to attack our lines."

"Or refuse to withdraw," Vernon added.

He had, Edmund thought, a damn good point. Those were Vernon's land, just over there, just across the river.

Vlod and the captain hitched two horses to the carriage of the last weapon in line, the one at the river end. The wagon had a plank for a seat, but it would do.

As they were connecting the traces, Ziellottes galloped out through the Gate.

It was a heaven-sent opportunity.

"I'll be right back," Vlod said.

He jumped down from the wagon and sprinted toward the spy. Waving his arms above his head, he shouted for him to stop.

Ziellottes reined in. "What is it?"

It was, perhaps, the one and only time Vlod had ever seen the old spy on edge, abrupt.

"I need you to carry a message to Ulricka."

"Do you have it?"

"I'll have to write it."

"Impossible," Ziellottes said. "I don't have the time."

The spy's horse was skittering back and forth. Its hooves pawing up tufts of grass.

"Will you have the time to help count the dead?"

After the briefest of hesitations, Ziellottes said, "Very well, little magus, but be quick."

———

Edmund refined the focus of his telescope. "Now they've moved over to one of the weapons. What's Vlod doing?"

"He's your magus," Vernon said, "but I suggest you leave him alone and see what comes of it."

"He's writing on a piece of paper."

"Obedient, isn't he?" Wolfram said. "Off on a tear, just like his father."

Vernon said, "If he weren't, he wouldn't be of any value."

———

While Ziellottes waited, Vlod wrote out his message to Ulricka.

When he had finished, he folded its two sheets into a packet and handed it to Ziellottes. "She must read that *before* she answers Edmund's response. *Before*, not after."

"You're not asking much," Ziellottes said, with unabashed sarcasm.

"I know what I'm asking. Do you?"

"You arrogant little bastard."

"Thorian was right, and Aerian was right," Vlod said. "Edmund can't use these new weapons, but neither can he give Narmer control of the river bar. The Two Lands must remain a fever dream."

"You'd like the planets to hang on a chain around your neck, too, wouldn't you?"

Vlod shook his head. "Too heavy."

Ziellottes laughed and spurred his horse toward the Mother Metropolitan's section of the enemy lines.

A bovine bawl attracted Vlod's attention. The lieutenant and a drover had arrived with the two steers. The animals looked out of sorts and bored.

Well, not for long.

———

Edmund slammed his fist onto the railing. "What's he doing?"

Far below and several meters along the wall toward the river, an ungainly detachment had separated from Vlod's unit. The detachment was making its way ponderously out into the space between the opposing armies.

Vlod and his unit's captain were riding on the carriage of one of the new weapons. The weapon's crew, presumably, complete with one of the unit's lieutenants, were walking beside it. Two steers had been tethered to the carriage and were following along behind. A drover trudged beside the two beasts.

The assemblage would have been comic if it hadn't been so ridiculous. Ridiculous was bad enough, but what made it dangerous was the fact that Vlod was headed straight for Ulricka's lines.

"Runner!" Edmund called.

Eighteen

Once Ziellottes was within the welcoming embrace of Ulricka's makeshift sitting room, with the door flap securely closed, he handed over Vlod's message.

"What about Edmund?" Ulricka asked. "What did he say?"

"Deal with Vlod's note first."

"Why? Has he offered to give himself up?"

"I doubt it," Ziellottes said.

"We shall see," Ulricka said. She opened the packet. "Two pages! What has he sent me? An epic poem?"

"Closer to a last will and testament, I should imagine."

Ulricka smoothed the sheets and read. "He writes a neat hand, for a man. Very readable." After a few seconds, she gave a little gasp and levered herself to her feet. The papers fell to the carpet.

"Shabnan!" Ulricka yelled.

Ziellottes winced.

"Shabnan!"

This time her shout had genuine alarm in it.

Against his better judgment, Ziellottes felt a blush of sympathy for her.

Shabnan rushed in. "Your Beatitude?" She glared at Ziellottes as though he may have distressed her beloved Mother Metropolitan.

"I'm riding onto the field," Ulricka said. "Summon horses for the two of us. No guards. Not one! And fetch Narmer. Desmond, too. It's time that alcoholic weasel earned his keep."

"You're too far along to ride on horseback."

"Stop making up excuses! If the pharaoh won't come with you, slit his throat!"

Shabnan's eyes flashed, but Ziellottes couldn't tell whether it was from surprise or anticipation. Was she praying for swift horses and Narmer's obedience, or for a sharp knife and a free and open path to Narmer's jugular?

"Yes, Your Beatitude," Shabnan said. She bowed low, a rarity as far as Ziellottes was aware, and ran—ran!—from the sitting room.

Shabnan's demand for horses filled the forecourt.

"What sort of a man is Vlod?" Ulricka asked. She changed into riding clothes, heedless of Ziellottes. "I've met him, but that's not saying much. The magi are a closed lot."

"He's quick. Ruthless. Dangerous. One of Yokashima's star pupils." Ziellottes added, "Principled."

"Doubly dangerous, then," Ulricka said. "Perhaps I ought to have burned him when I had the chance."

"You would have come to despise yourself for it," Ziellottes said.

"Nothing good can come from dishonor? That old tag?"

"If you like. Put it this way. If you had burned him, you would have lost my respect."

Ulricka's face went white.

Had she never guessed?

No, he did not love her, no part of it, but he did respect her. She did her job, her impossible job, better than most had done it, and against overwhelming odds, too, and for that he held her in high regard.

Shabnan reappeared. "The horses are ready, Your Beatitude, and Narmer and Desmond are coming."

Ulricka hurried out, leaving Ziellottes alone in the room.

He waited silently until they had ridden off, until the guards had resumed their routine, and then, with slow, smooth movements, he picked up the two discarded sheets of paper.

Vlod heard the shouts. They were coming from behind: a rider was approaching.

The captain cast a worried look over his shoulder.

"Keep going," Vlod said. "He'll catch up in no time."

Less than a minute later the rider was beside the carriage. He said, "My lord Edmund sends his compliments and directs you to return the weapon to its assigned location and to report to him immediately."

"Please convey my respects to my lord Edmund. Please inform him that I am about to determine whether our new weapons will make suitable skirmishing devices. I am conducting a vital weapons test in place, under potentially live battlefield conditions. Therefore, it would be inconvenient for me to comply with his request at this time. I would, however, deem it a distinct honor if he were to witness the test in person."

Ulricka was mounted sidesaddle on a large stallion. He was jigging this way and that, tired of standing, anxious to run. The horse gave her a sense of both comfort and power. Shabnan was next to her, also mounted sidesaddle, on a no-less-spirited mare. The two women's skirts hung in vivid sweeps of the primary colors. The toes of their highly polished boots shone black in the sun.

Narmer, his battlemaster, and a gaggle of attendants rode up to them.

Ulricka frowned at him. "I sent for you, not your underlings."

"What's this about?" Narmer asked. "I have a battle to win."

"It hasn't started yet," Ulricka said.

Of Shabnan, she asked, "Where's Desmond?"

"He's on his way, Your Beatitude."

Ulricka returned her attention to Narmer. She fixed him with what she hoped was a cold glare. "Your bootlickers are still here. Send them away."

Narmer flushed, but he turned to his retinue, and said, "Continue the inspection without me."

The gaggle made regretful noises, but rode back in the direction from which they'd come.

Ulricka took out her telescope and scanned the prospective battlefield.

Out in the middle distance, between the two armies, a wagon, men-at-arms, a drover and two steers, and Vlod were making slow-but-steady progress toward her lines.

Her lines. She had to remember that they were *her* lines, not Narmer's. He may have fielded the larger army, but it was her moral sanction that had allowed their combined forces to move downriver, and it was her spiritual leadership that would provide the impetus to conquer Edmund, Vernon, and their allies.

Desmond rode up. "Your Beatitude," he said, and bowed. His eyes were red-rimmed, and he stank of yesterday's liquor and last night's anal intercourse. "What's ado?"

"Never mind what. Just stay in company," Ulricka said, and spurred her horse forward.

The party followed her.

Her stomach was churning again, so she was careful to ride upwind from Desmond.

"A skirmishing weapon! Inconvenient!" Edmund shouted. "Does he think I've gone senile?"

The rider shrank inside his uniform. "I've repeated his words exactly, my lord."

Wolfram said, "None of us doubts it, lad."

Wolfram's behavior rankled Edmund. It was fine for Wolfram to play the calm, rational master of any situation. He had nothing clinging to his shoulders but the outcome of the occasional battle. It was Edmund who had to decide whether to fight them, Edmund who had to raise the armies and assemble the matériel, Edmund who had to ensure the navigation channels remained open, and Edmund who had to hold Clan Iredale together no matter what befell it.

War, peace, plenty, famine—none of it excused failure.

Nor did disobedient magi.

Failure was failure, and failure inevitably meant death.

Did Vlod take Edmund for some idiot stableboy?

Edmund wrestled himself away from the tirade. He was being grossly unfair *and* he was clouding his judgement. He wished confusion to the enemy, not to himself. He needed to be as clear-headed as possible, as calm as possible, as determined as possible. He thanked the Gods and the Generations that he had kept his adolescent tantrum to himself.

Vernon gestured with his telescope toward the middle of the field, between the two armies. To Edmund, he said, "You might want to have a look."

Edmund opened his telescope and trained it where Vernon had indicated.

Vlod was using a long wooden lever to train one of the new weapons in the direction of the hills to the west. At the same time, a drover was leading a steer to the west.

To the west?

Why to the west?

No, Edmund realized with a shock, that wasn't at all what the drover was doing.

The drover was leading the steer *downrange*.

Edmund had been blind not to have seen what Vlod was doing, from the outset. Damn Aerian! Damn him and his notions of demonstration! Of fair warning!

That trumped-up shit Narmer didn't deserve a warning, and neither did Ulricka!

How in hell had things come to this pass?

He didn't have far to look for an answer. The Iredales sat athwart the mouth of the river, a piece of real estate that was becoming more and more enviable with each passing year.

Well, Edmund thought, perhaps he ought to hand it over to them! Let them deal with the channels, the jetties, and the storm-tossed wrecks!

But he'd never do it. No, he wouldn't walk away.

Life wasn't that simple.

Narmer wouldn't be satisfied, he wouldn't stop, until he'd obliterated clan Iredale, not in name perhaps, but in fact.

And *that* Edmund would not allow, not while he had breath in him!

On the far side of the field a group of riders was approaching Vlod's position from the southeast. They were yet a good distance away, but they were coming up fast.

Edmund adjusted his telescope until he had the image as clear as the lenses would allow. His chest tightened as he recognized the riders: Ulricka, Shabnan, Narmer, and that filthy turncoat Desmond.

Edmund swore under his breath. He stalked toward the stairs. "Wolfram, you're with me. Vernon? Trevor? Care to join us?"

———

Ziellottes' hands trembled, rattling the paper so loudly that he was afraid the guards would hear and come to investigate.

Your Beatitude,
By now Desmond has told you about the new throwing engines Aerian and I have built. Your spies have added their observations. You have a store of information, but you do not yet have enough to make a hard-and-fast decision.

Ulricka had been right. Vlod did write a clean hand, and he wrote logically, too.

These new weapons ought to be of concern to you. They are of concern to me. So far we've called them the "new weapons, but they're nothing of the sort. They're ancient, and they are a stark violation of the Harmony. They stand at the root, or very near to it, of why the Goddess sent the Great Winter. They can—

Vlod was alluding to the opening cycle of the Second Creation. He was arguing that Edmund's new weapons were a current version of an ancient sin. But Vlod wouldn't have wasted his time on so self-evident a point. He must have had another line of argument in mind.

—smash troop formations at will, reduce men-at-arms to bloody piles of shredded flesh and broken bone, and send armies into headlong flight. They are able to batter down fortresses, sink ships, and hurl explosive charges into town centers. They kill at range, with neither hesitation nor regret nor mercy. They change warriors into machines. They reduce enemies to targets. They obliterate skill, courage, honor, and glory. Only the slaughter of war remains.

Ah, there was his other point: war and the honor of war. It seemed that Vlod was more a warrior-sage than he was a magus.

Their use will destroy warfare, but it will destroy religion as well. The cathedral, henges, pools, shrines, retreat houses, hermitages, monasteries, seminaries, and schools will fade into oblivion. I leave it to you to discern the causes.

Considering that the Cathedral had murdered his father, Vlod's concern for it was either generous to a fault or an agreeable oddity of his character. Or it could be that Vlod had attained a level of wisdom far beyond his years. Ziellottes was willing to put good money on the third option.

The new weapons are a blight. Therefore, you must act to prevent Edmund from using them. It is beyond my power to dissuade him. Only you can do it.

This part of the text was sloppy and emotional. Vlod sounded as if he were—because he was!—trapped in a cage of his own design and construction. No wonder it had taken him so long to compose his message.

If your forces attack, Edmund will have no choice but to order the use of the new weapons, and I will have no choice but to obey his order. I will do so willingly. No matter the ultimate costs, neither Edmund nor I can allow Narmer to enslave the Iredales. Therefore, you must withdraw.

Ulricka? Withdraw? Never. She may have read the note, and she may have rushed out into the field, but she was in no position to capitulate, nor was it in her to do so. She would bob and she would weave, but she would never surrender.

I will provide you with both proof of what I have said and a pretext to act as I have urged. Against Edmund's express orders, I will show you the new weapons in action. As soon as you can, join me in the middle of the field.

Come quickly. Bring whomever you wish, but not more than four or five. If we delay, Edmund will arrest me, and then, inevitably, the battle will be joined and the cathedral's forces will be destroyed.

Ziellottes shook his head in bewilderment. Vlod had promised—in writing!—to commit an act of treason.

No. That couldn't be. It was impossible to believe that Vlod was not acting on Edmund's orders. But in that case, why wouldn't Edmund have made the offer himself?

Or had Edmund laid a trap?

The false traitor was an old, old ploy. Doubtless Ulricka had taken Vlod's protestations seriously because she herself could not believe in the righteousness of Edmund's cause.

She believed that nothing but the highest of ideals motivated her, but she also believed that Edmund was driven by the lowest sorts of greed.

Under those circumstances, Vlod's betrayal of his chieftain, for that was what Edmund was, made perfect sense.

Assuming that it was a false-traitor gambit, was it Edmund's plan for Vlod to assassinate her?

Ziellottes pressed his mouth into a tight line.

No, that couldn't be.

Assassination wasn't the least bit like Edmund, nor would he send Vlod to his death in the service of such a suicidal nonsense.

Edmund, Wolfram, and Vlod had to be aware that Ulricka never did so much as go to the privy without five or six attendants.

But she had taken no such number with her. Shabnan, Desmond, and Narmer, those were her companions.

No, no, no, their intent could not be assassination—unless Vlod himself did not intend to survive, which made no sense whatsoever. Edmund would never allow such stupidity, such waste.

Could their conspiracy have penetrated into the heart of Ulricka's inner circle? Did Edmund have agents in place to help matters along?

The idea was not inconceivable.

In recent weeks, Ziellottes had picked up a hint or two that Xenia was flirting with the idea that she could usurp Ulricka's place. Perhaps Xenia had enlisted Edmund in her cause. She'd been friendly enough with Vernon over the last while. He might well have served as her route to Edmund.

Ziellottes shook his head in an uncomfortable mélange of confusion, frustration, and consternation. When it came to the issue at hand, the gears in the cause-and-effect machine of power politics were refusing to mesh as they ought to.

Vlod an assassin?

It was out of the question.

To put it baldly, neither Edmund nor Vlod were that stupid.

Ziellottes returned his attention to the note. He had raced ahead of himself. It was better not to speculate. An explanation might lie in the next few lines.

Edmund's use of the new weapons will make me a heretic by commission, in that I made it possible for him to do so. If you do not act to prevent it, Edmund's use of the new weapons will make you a heretic by omission, in that you will have made it possible for him to do so by having done nothing to prevent it.

Despite the rhetorical tangle, Vlod had constructed a delightfully logical moral trap. Ulricka could not condemn Vlod unless she also condemned herself.

Her one escape was the old plea that she could not be held responsible for the actions of another. Which was true enough.

Except for the fact that she did have it within her power to prevent Edmund's actions. Thus her inaction, her refusal, would constitute an action. She would act by not acting. She would commit heresy by not preventing Edmund and Vlod from committing heresy.

That line of reasoning was a bloody road and no mistake, but a road it was, complete with mileposts and convenient wayside charnel houses.

Together, we will have violated the Harmony and plunged the Inland Empire and the Holy Oregon into a wretched and bloody struggle. They will fight and die without hope, without honor, and without purpose. As a consequence, we will stand rightly and irrevocably condemned.

Therefore, I beg you to join me as soon as possible on the patch of bottomland between the armies.

—Vlod, Magus to Edmund

Ziellottes let out a slow, frightened breath.

Condemned.

Condemned of the same abomination that had caused the Goddess to send the Great Winter in the first place.

Had humanity learned nothing?

Apparently not.

The prospect wrenched his soul.

Ziellottes replaced the note on the floor.

No wonder Ulricka had run from her pavilion.

The door opened and a guard entered the room. She glared at him as though he were a rotten animal carcass. "I thought I heard someone. You don't belong in here."

"I'm just leaving," Ziellottes said, and dodged around her.

Luckily, she made no move to stop him. He didn't have time for the niceties of question and answer.

Xenia, Seldon's sister, focused her telescope on Vlod and his merry band of jolly warriors.

Unless she was quite mistaken, they were manhandling a wagon. In its bed was a length of what looked like a bundle of iron-bound wooden boards.

With a sense of cold dread, Xenia realized that those insignificant boards had to be part of Vlod's so-called new weapon, his gunpowder-fired throwing engine.

According to the reports she'd received—either directly or via her brother—the iron-bound strips reinforced a length of iron pipe, capped at one end and open at the other.

It wasn't the pipe that was important, but what came out of it...at tremendous velocity and with a murderous amount of force.

Gunpowder, of course, was the culprit. The reports had verged on the hysterical on that point. They'd wailed as though gunpowder were the bane of civilized life.

It could be, but not when handled properly and put to the proper uses. During festivals and the like, it could be an unequalled delight. It lit up the sky in a burst and shower of vibrant colors. The *Booms* echoing. The poignant fading of color, the diminishment of light. Until the next flash, the next explosion of color, the next raucous, joy-filled *Boom*.

That was not, she suspected, the sorts of explosions and flashes Edmund's magus had in mind. Not the sorts of color, either. Blood red, bone white, the off-white of intestines, the pink of muscle tissue—those were more the run of colors Vlod was hoping to create.

A noise farther along the line attracted Xenia's attention.

Ulricka, Shabnan, that wretched oaf Narmer, and someone she almost recognized—short, overweight, and oily—rode out between the units.

Xenia had seen short-and-oily around the encampment, but couldn't place him.

Could he be that traitorous magus Desmond?

Yes, he had to be.

The riders formed into a group and then, with Ulricka in the lead, galloped off toward the middle of the field. Too bad they weren't chasing a fox or a feral dog.

She refocused her telescope on Edmund's intrepid magus and his audacious band of loveable miscreants.

And they were loveable: the Mother Metropolitan would love to watch them play hopscotch, each of them at the end of his very own rope.

By this time, they'd swung the wagon around and had brought it to a stop. The strip-bound pipe was pointing to the west.

One of Vlod's people unhitched the horses and led them away to the northeast, while another, who could only be a drover, led a cow—no, a steer!—toward the hills to the west.

The drover carried a sledgehammer and an iron stake. Did he intend to slaughter it, the poor dear? No, that wasn't likely.

If one and one made two—and they usually did—then a far worse fate was in store for the steer, the poor, deprived thing.

Given what catapult-thrown rocks could do to tethered animals, she shuddered to envision what Vlod's new weapon could do. The steer might literally explode due to the force of the impact. There'd be nothing recognizable left but the head, part of the neck, the four legs, the tail. The rest would be nothing but offal, shattered bones, and jagged pieces of muscle tissue.

Oh, and a large puddle of blood, of course.

The stench of torn intestines, too.

Most of all, she remembered that about her brother's experiment. The stench.

On another subject, did steers lament the loss of their testicles? Did they miss them? Pine away for them on cold, lonely nights? Did they even know? Were they aware?

Xenia wondered about that.

She doubted it.

The majority of Seldon's people didn't seem to mind in the least.

Castrati, the lot of them.

Perhaps her brother hadn't used a knife on their private parts—most of the time, anyway—but he'd castrated them sure enough. They were barely able to grow facial hair, or maintain an erection, or think for themselves, and damn few of them ever objected.

As far as Xenia could tell, they didn't care one way or the other. Yes, my lord. No, my lord. Immediately, my lord. To serve you is my joy, my lord.

Xenia pointed at Vlod's wagon, and said to her brother: "We ought to join the party."

Seldon lowered his telescope. "The Mother Metropolitan didn't invite us. Remember, I'm a very junior partner in this alliance, which is the way I want it."

Perhaps he was the castrato.

"You don't know what you want," Xenia said, and urged her horse forward.

Her brother let out a string of oaths, but followed along like a good boy.

As they came out onto the open ground between the armies, Xenia noticed that Ziellottes, that delightful, old spy, had pointed himself toward the wagon, too. She wondered who else would be in attendance.

Nineteen

Vlod stood between Ulricka, who was seated on a camp stool, and Edmund, who was seated on his horse.

Shabnan, Narmer, Vernon, Wolfram, Ziellottes, Desmond, and several others had gathered around.

The day had remained fair, and it was possible to catch the silt-heavy scent of the river, flowing sluggishly in high summer.

The fall rains would put a stop to that, restoring the river's volume and strength.

A dozen meters away, one of the weapon's crewmen pulled the rammer out of the weapon's muzzle, the open end of the wood-bound iron pipe. The rammer was a pole about the length and width of a broom handle. It had a wooden plug attached to one end, which gave it the look of a pump piston.

The crews used the rammer to seat the charge, wad, and shot against the closed end of the tube.

"They're almost ready," Vlod said.

Downrange, a rider from Vlod's unit was warning Edmund's skirmishers, sending them off to the north or south, not far, but far enough.

"I thought you dragged me out here to see a terrible weapon," Ulricka said. She was in as much form as her pregnancy would allow. "What you've shown me so far is a length of pipe mounted on a cut-down farm wagon."

"The terrible weapon will arrive shortly, Your Beatitude," Vlod said.

Ulricka looked pale and exhausted. She wasn't overdue, but it wouldn't be much longer. She was, Vlod guessed, likely to complete her return to the cathedral without incident, but her baby would be arriving soon after.

Edmund exchanged idle comments with Ulricka.

Ziellottes was quiet, not sullen, not angry, but—could it be? —worried.

Desmond stood apart. He was jittery, his face pale, eyes darting. As soon as he could, he'd be climbing into the nearest bottle.

Vlod decided that Desmond looked terrified. He ought to. If he hadn't arrived under Ulricka's protection, Vlod, if not Wolfram, if not Edmund himself, would have plunged a knife through the drunken bastard's heart.

Weeks ago Vlod had decided that only Desmond could have blown up the powder shack and with it Eakan, Vlod's foreman.

Narmer pointed toward his and Ulricka's line, toward two approaching riders. "What do *they* want?" he asked. Disgust dripped from every syllable.

"Who?" Ulricka asked.

"Our uninvited guests," Narmer said.

A man and a woman rode at a swift but unhurried pace across the open ground. They were armed, but they were dressed more for a military review than for a war.

"Seldon and Xenia," Wolfram said.

Vernon said, "In the flesh."

"This was supposed to have been between the grownups," Ulricka said.

"They are grownups," Vernon said.

"Who says?" Ulricka asked.

"Their army," Vernon said.

"*His* army," Narmer said.

"Opinions differ," Vernon said.

Vlod agreed with Vernon, but didn't say so publicly. It wasn't his place.

An exchange of instructions drew his attention to the weapon.

The captain produced a mason's level and checked the weapon's elevation. They would fire at what amounted to pointblank range, so an elevation check was largely a matter of show. He checked the measured angle against a chart, nodded his satisfaction, and stepped aside.

Downrange, the drover was feeding the steer, which moments before, he had tethered to the iron stake. A bucket of water sat within the animal's easy reach.

Did either the steer or the drover have any idea what was about to happen? The steer couldn't, not beyond a vague sense of threat, if that much. The animal was too busy eating to care about much of anything else. But the drover had to have some idea of what was about to happen. He couldn't possibly be so naïve as not to.

Then again, why not? No one had witnessed the sort of event that was about to happen in over six hundred years, and it had been precious few back then.

Seldon and Xenia dismounted and handed their horses' reins to one of Vlod's men-at-arms, who tethered the animals with the rest of the horses.

Careful to ensure her sword and battle knife didn't foul, Xenia bowed and then stooped to kiss Ulricka on both cheeks. It was a cheekbone-to-cheekbone kiss, with lips puckering in empty air and the cheekbones never touching.

Xenia straightened up. "Your Beatitude, please forgive us. We can't apologize enough for our tardiness. Your messenger must have lost her way. The layout of the camp confuses a lot of people."

"I'm sure she'll turn up," Ulricka said.

"Well, what's happening?" Xenia asked. She fixed Narmer with an unenthralled look. "Which one of you intends to tell the leader of one third of your army why we're here? Personally, I couldn't care less, but my brother is absolutely agog to find out." She darted over to the weapon and climbed up onto its carriage. Her skirts billowed in the wind. "What have we here? Why, it must be one of those new thingies everyone's been fussing about? It looks like a length of sewer pipe to me, but what do I know? I never was much good at any of the industrial arts. Couldn't find the time for them. Too much politics and sex, I guess." She showered her most radiant smile on Vlod. "Tell me, what on earth have you built?"

Beneath her calculated tone, her deliberate, flamboyant stupidity, Vlod detected hidden layers of concern and respect. He decided to answer. "A new sort of throwing engine."

"The ancients had such devices, sort of," Xenia said. "Didn't they?"

"They did," Vlod said.

"Why, I do believe that I shall be obliged to watch your every move. You are a wicked, wicked man. You've dug up one of the old heresies, haven't you?"

"I do what I can."

"I'm sure you do."

Xenia turned to Narmer. "I do so hate to miss a picnic."

"I—" Narmer began.

Xenia cut him off. "We're here now. No harm done. No need to apologize, unless it would make you feel better. Would it?" She walked over to Vernon and looked up into his face.

Vlod read the gesture as an open display of affection or, at least, sexual desire. Was it, however, the affection of a woman for the man she loves, or was it the affection of a cougar for the stag it intends to devour?

"It's time for the entertainment, isn't it?" she asked.

"You're incorrigible," Vernon said.

"I do love a good show."

Vernon's grin widened.

"Don't we all," Shabnan said, her tone dripping acid.

Vlod signaled the captain, who faced downrange and waved a flag. The drover waved his arms, patted the steer, and ran back to stand with the weapon's crew.

"Ready to fire," the captain reported.

Vlod lit a long-handled torch and approached the weapon.

The steer lifted its head and seemed to focus on the torch.

"We thank you for your life," Vlod said, and pressed the torch down onto the tiny mound of gunpowder on top of the touchhole.

Flame and smoke flared upwards, and the open end of the tube erupted in flame, smoke, and sound. The weapon kicked back, and the wheels of its carriage shrieked.

Vlod and his crews hadn't had much time to practice with the new weapons, but they had taught themselves the basics of training and elevation.

The projectile struck with savage force, far worse than the impact of a mechanically thrown rock of the same size.

At the same time, the detonation echoed from the bluff and from the line of hills to the west.

The central portion of the steer's body on its downrange side exploded outward in a spray of shattered bone, lengths of viscera, and blood.

The beast bawled out, but only for an instant. Blood and stomach contents geysered up its throat and choked off the sound. What had begun as a scream ended as a strangled grunt.

The bull Vlod had sacrificed and augured to determine the outcome of a marriage between Dagna and Gregory had fared far, far better.

The steer's legs buckled, and it fell to the ground. It kicked and thrashed. Jets of blood and pink froth ran from its mouth.

After exiting the steer's body, the projectile, its force spent, followed a shallow, downward arc.

The steer convulsed and died.

The projectile touched the ground, skipped a few times, and came to rest in a patch of dirt where a squad of Edmund's skirmishers had cleared a place for a cooking fire.

Less than a second had separated Vlod's order to fire and the steer's death.

Shabnan gasped in disbelief.

Her involuntary intake of breath snapped Vlod out of the mechanics of the demonstration. A shudder wracked his body, and it took an act of will for him not to scream like a madman and run off into the trees.

Perhaps the Cathedral had been right to burn his father!

"The second steer?" Ulricka asked.

Vlod wrestled his emotions into silence. "I brought it in case you believed the first shot to have been a lucky one," he said. "Shall we reload and fire again?"

"That won't be necessary," Ulricka said.

"Good," Xenia said. "I'm sick of stew."

"How about soup?" Seldon said.

"Kebabs would be a treat," Vernon said.

TWENTY

And kebabs it was but not immediately and not entirely. Other matters, matters of life and death, took precedence.

Under Shabnan's watchful, irksome gaze, Ulricka lowered herself into the most comfortable chair in her pavilion. It was a straight-backed affair with generous arms and deep cushions.

Shabnan handed her a cup of tea. It was hot and cut the chill that had crept into her despite the day's warmth, but it did nothing to dispel her memory of how the runt's weapon had blown the steer apart.

How had the ancients faced such abominations? How had they inflicted such slaughter on one another? How could they have thought of themselves as moral and upright and just?

The rot must have twisted them, deformed them to their very souls.

Inventions like that, now rediscovered, proved the wisdom of the Second Creation.

Ulricka took a second sip of her tea.

The jaws of hell had reopened, right in front of her.

Hell. That word was making the rounds these days, and rightly so. The Inland Empire and the Holy Oregon teetered on its brink.

The slightest misstep and they were bound to plunge.

The logic behind the weapon was undeniable. No clan volunteered for extinction. Life was about survival.

The death of an *individual* was acceptable, in that death was a stage in the journey from this shadow of life to the true life that awaited with the Gods and the Generations. The death of an *entire people* was intolerable. There were exceptions. There were always—

Ulricka stopped herself. Her platitudes were ridiculously self-serving.

Cannons.

There. She'd used the word. Now she could be done with the pussy-footing.

Cannons: the ancient scourge.

Was it possible Edmund would be as demonic as to unleash them?

Yes.

It was preposterous to assume that he would not. Narmer's attack would leave him no choice, and Narmer was sure to attack. The logic of his geography necessitated it.

Shabnan poured Ulricka a refill.

Ulricka sipped it, but the tea had grown bitter in the pot. She set her cup off to one side. She had work to do.

"Fetch the Cathedral's augur," she said. "Do it quietly."

"Yes, Your Beatitude," Shabnan said, and left.

One of Ulricka's attendants caught the flap and poked her head in. She had fixed her face in an anticipatory expression: upturned lips, raised eyebrows, wide eyes. She was the picture of a sycophant, mindless and eager-to-help, the quintessential toady.

Ulricka was tempted to throw the teapot at her.

"Thank you, but I need to be alone," Ulricka said.

The face retained its subservient mask, but the head to which it was attached nodded. "Yes, Your Beatitude. Thank you, Your Beatitude," the mouth said. Finally, the head, the mouth, the eyes, and—blessing of bless-ings!—that ghastly, mindless expression disappeared from view.

The flap dropped back into place.

Ulricka closed her eyes.

Vlod was a dangerous whore. There wasn't a magus who wasn't a whore, but that runt knew his business.

Ulricka thought back to what had happened after Seldon had made his humorous suggestion about soup and Vernon had countered with kebabs.

The crows and the gulls had descended and set to squabbling over the carcass, even before it had stopped bleeding.

In other circumstances, they would have begun their pecking and ripping before their victim was dead, at the moment meaningful resistance was no longer possible.

Maybe that was the point, to begin while the meat was fresh, to begin before the larger scavengers had laid their claims.

To Vlod, Narmer had said, "I'm not about to turn tail and run."

"Open your eyes," Vlod said.

Edmund began to speak, but Wolfram put a hand on his brother's arm, persuading him not to.

To Vlod, Narmer was saying, "Your gunpowder trinkets cannot stop an army, not any army of mine!"

"We have several of such *trinkets*, and together they can stop *enough* of your army," Vlod said.

"I'm not about to shit my pants at the idea that men-at-arms die in battle."

"Then promise me," Vlod said, "that you'll be in the front rank when the hankie drops."

That modest request sent the would-be conqueror of the Columbia River Basin into a red-faced rant.

When it was over, Vlod asked politely, "Does that mean you'll lead the charge or not?"

"It means I'll use your guts for harp strings," Narmer shouted. Spittle flew from his mouth. The stringy droplets sparkled in the sun.

"You're free to try," Vlod said, "but I've never been especially musical." He continued to Ulricka: "A middle ground is possible, Your Beatitude. If Edmund agrees, the Cathedral could establish a neutral commission to *advise* on the operation of the river bar." Vlod left a pause. "In the absence of an agreement, Edmund could build hundreds of his new weapons and use them to replace you."

"You're insane!" Narmer yelled.

Shabnan joined in. "How dare—"

Ulricka cut them off with a wave of her hand. "Replace me on what basis?"

"Your subordination of the Cathedral to a cabal of heretical upriver clans," Vlod said.

"I'm no—"

"You most certainly are," Vlod said. "You're besotted with pharaonic spirituality. You would rather worship Amun-Ra than the Great Goddess." Vlod smiled a knowing smile. "I suspect that in private you already do."

Narmer began yelling, but Ulricka cut him off. To Vlod, she said, "Tell me, magus, do you have anyone in mind to take my place?"

"A milkmaid would do."

"A milkmaid?"

"Why not? Every new mother metropolitan has to learn her role—the important parts of it, anyway—from scratch."

"Don't be coy," Ulricka said. "You must have a name."

Another knowing smile inched across Vlod's face.

"The *who* is unimportant. Anyone would do," Vlod said. He waved in Xenia's direction. "Take Xenia for example. She's a henge dancer. She's devout, attractive enough to interest a year king, and she's young enough to have children for years to come. How about Xenia? Yes, come to think of it, why not Xenia?"

Ulricka expected Xenia to express at least a politic level of surprise, but Ulricka could find no trace of surprise, or of denial, on the woman's face.

To Xenia, Ulricka said, "Don't push too hard. It's unbecoming."

"Your Beatitude, I have no desire to replace you," Xenia said.

How easily, but how clumsily, she lied!

To the group at large, Ulricka said: "We shall resume over dinner in my pavilion tonight."

The chieftains had wanted to slaughter one another then and there, but given Ulricka's moral authority, they had consented to hold off.

Her standing hadn't been enough to cow Edmund and Vernon, let alone Narmer, into submission, but it had been enough to delay the battle. Her standing had done the trick, but so had the immediacy of the steer's blood soaking into the ground, its mangled body strewn hither and yon across it.

How far the chunks had flown!

The group fragmented, began to drift away.

In an aside to Shabnan, Ulricka said, "Post a guard over the steer's carcass. They're to keep the scavengers away. I want that animal left exactly as it is now."

"Yes, Your Beatitude," Shabnan said. "As it is, where it is, until you say otherwise."

"Exactly."

Now, in the sitting room of her pavilion, Ulricka tried to decide whether to call for a pot of coffee—anything to wash away the taste of that slovenly tea.

Vlod, the little prick, had upstaged Edmund. The thought of it sent tremors of delight through her. The runt had overplayed his hand, though, and Edmund would never forgive him for it.

That breach alone might be enough to topple the Iredales.

The flap eased back and one of her guards entered. "The augur is here, Your Beatitude."

"Show him in," Ulricka said, "and bring coffee."

————————————————

Edmund and Wolfram were alone on the field. They were riding slowly back toward the main gate. They were away from any ears but their own. The sky was blue, the morning's indolent breeze had died away to nothing, and the air smelled of sun-warmed trees and armies standing on tiptoes, of freshly oiled steel, and of recently dug latrines.

"I killed Thorian for less!" Edmund said.

"Killing him was a mistake," Wolfram said.

"It would have been worse to have left him alive."

"True," Wolfram said, but he had his doubts on that score. Would it have been any worse than a third of Edmund's allies weighing whether to withdraw from the field? Worse than a second third of them mulling over whether to change sides altogether? Worse than a score of grieving relatives cherishing revenge against Edmund and the Iredales?

"Vlod pulled us back from the edge," Wolfram said. "Would you rather have your men-at-arms dead?"

"No, I wouldn't," Edmund grumbled. "I'm not a fool."

"Then you have to smile and pretend that he acted on your orders."

"Success absolves?"

"It will be *your* victory."

"Don't appeal to my vanity."

"Why not? You are vain," Wolfram said. "If Vlod succeeds, we win. If he fails, we engage the enemy and fight through to a glorious victory."

Edmund's shoulders slumped.

The storm had passed.

"What's next?" Edmund asked.

"We enjoy the respite. We attend the Mother Metropolitan's dinner. We negotiate the best possible treaty." Wolfram shrugged. "Then we go home. We rebuild your alliances and we find new ones. We redouble your forces."

"Walls and stores?"

"Cannons and gunpowder."

Ceremonial or not, Xenia's armor was heavy and hot, and she wanted out of it. Summer had its attractions, but it was not the season to run around encased in leather and steel.

Vlod's demonstration had taken place at least an hour ago, and Xenia's horse continued to shy at the slightest sound. A bird, a dog, a squirrel—it didn't seem to matter. The slightest bit of chatter caused him to rear his head and flare his nostrils.

Xenia leaned forward and patted his neck. She bathed him in soft-spoken nonsense: "You're such a good old horse. You'd make a fine pot of glue. Pot after pot of fine, fine glue. Yes, you would. You would, you would, you would. And if you don't settle down pretty soon, I'm going to cut off a tree branch and beat you with it until your eyes cross. On the other hand, if you behave, I'll give you a carrot dipped in sugar. You'd like that, wouldn't you? A carrot dipped in sugar? I know I would."

She wished the same technique would work on her brother when he was out of sorts, which he was now. Her life would be so much happier if she could pat Seldon's neck, coo to him, and feed him a carrot. Unfortunately, her brother was too much like the opposite end of a horse.

They were riding on the top of the earthwork that bordered the river, heading south. They had water to their left, and down on the flat to their right were wild rhododendrons, dense-packed cottonwoods, and blackberry vines, huge banks of them. The aroma of the berries hung over the earthwork.

A pie?

What a marvelous idea!

Should she embrace domesticity, her much-neglected distaff side, and pick berries and bake a pie?

The idea of it had its attractions. She could share the pie with her horse. He'd earned it, unlike her brother. Her horse would slurp it right down and beg for more, the Greedy Gus.

"Sorry to drag you out here," Seldon said.

"You have your reasons," Xenia said.

"We can't afford to be overheard."

"What's so important?"

"Are you angling to be the next mother metropolitan?"

"No."

It was a blatant lie. For the last several months, she'd been doing nothing else.

At the moment, however, she wasn't so sure. Ulricka's current pregnancy stood a good chance of killing her, and rather than stay in her apartments where she belonged, she had taken the field with the Cathedral Guard.

She'd had no choice in the matter, but from the medical point of view, she ought not to have done it. She ought to have stayed safe and sound at the cathedral.

It had been another one of those countless choices the office made for its incumbent.

Ulricka's life was a dreary schedule of festivals, rites, duties, ritual copulation, and pregnancies. It was a round without end, until the inevitable day when her court declared that she hadn't conceived one too many years in a row, or that she was going through menopause, or that she'd given birth to a third weakling, and that, therefore, it was time for the Province of the Inland Empire and the Holy Oregon of the North American Communion to elect her successor and for her successor to strike her down.

Hack, slash, chop, plop.

Off you go, dear.

May you find the serenity in the next life that eluded you in this life!

So much for any hope of a graceful old age.

Sorry, honey, but you've dried up, outlived your usefulness, grown *old*. Old—all well and good in a crone, but *not* in a mother metropolitan.

Repeating herself, Xenia said, "No, I have no desire to become the Mother Metropolitan." She gave her horse a final pat, and straightened up.

"Then why does the overgrown urchin think you do?"

She glared at her brother. "He doesn't. He pulled my name out of his ass."

"You'll have to make nice with Ulricka."

"Yes, I imagine I will."

Perhaps a blackberry pie would do...

Before her brother could burden her with a list of infantile instructions, Xenia wheeled her horse around and spurred it into a full gallop. It was time for the two of them to burn off the dregs of a squalid morning.

Barkley, the augur, held his body bent forward and kept his eyebrows raised in an expression of attentive expectation. He reminded Ulricka of a shopkeeper waiting on a belligerent customer.

Ulricka said, "Vlod—"

Barkley nodded his recognition.

"—has built a number of gunpowder-powered throwing engines, cannons. Earlier today, he used one of them to kill a steer."

Barkley's attentive expression remained unchanged. "I heard about it. A dreadful business, Your Beatitude."

"I want you to augur the carcass. Once you have, the butchers will collect it. I intend to serve it at a dinner I'm hosting tonight."

"The steer is not to be thanked for its life and cremated?"

"Vlod will perform the necessary rites. The head will be cremated in token of the entire body."

"Forgive me, Your Beatitude, but I'm confused. Why serve it at a dinner?"

"I want the manner of the steer's death to strike deep."

Barkley inclined his head. "The augury? What is your question?"

This was the hardest part of any augury. Each began with a question. It had to. Otherwise, a psychic fog obscured the revelation.

"Vlod's cannons have changed everything," Ulricka said. "Their use in battle will call down the wrath of the Goddess."

"How so?"

"You can't be that stupid!"

"I've never seen a cannon fired," he said. "It would be dangerous for me to assume I comprehend that which I do not."

Ulricka explained.

When she'd finished, Barkley said, "The stories were correct, then."

"You understand."

"That much and a sliver more."

Barkley drew himself up. He squared his shoulders and dropped his obsequious attitude. His eyes brightened and the line of his mouth hardened.

Where, Ulricka wondered, had the man thus revealed been hiding? *Why* had he been hiding?

"What sliver?" she asked.

Without asking her permission, Barkley sat down. He leaned forward and rested his elbows on his knees. His eyes took on a fierce glint.

"Vlod is not a bad person," he said. "He demonstrated the power of his cannons in order to protect the Harmony."

"He claims as much," Ulricka said, "in a letter delivered this morning."

"You don't believe him?"

"Wasn't that demonstration Edmund's idea? Wasn't he using the runt as a blind to protect himself?"

"I'd be flabbergasted if Edmund had been. Edmund has limitless courage, but he is not a deep thinker. Vlod is."

"He's a tinkerer."

Barkley smiled one of those infuriating smiles magi were prone to display. It was like a child's taunt: *I know something you don't know! I know something you don't know!*

He asked, "How did you react when you saw what happened to the steer?"

"I wanted to throw up."

"He warned you, didn't he?"

"Yes, he did," she said, making it a very human confession.

"Imagine how much worse it would have been if that steer had been your army."

"That was the whole point of the exercise, and, yes, I have imagined it."

"Good. Therefore, what is your question?"

"What would you ask?" She was out of her depth, floundering, and didn't mind if he witnessed it.

"I'm not you," he said.

"Pretend."

Barkley sat back and steepled his fingers. It was one of his more pompous, irritating gestures. His eyes went out of focus, and he closed them, as though he couldn't think properly with them open.

After several seconds, she asked, "Well?"

Barkley opened his eyes. They were blue, and they sprang into focus like two cocked and loaded crossbows.

"If I were you," he said, "I would ask, 'Is my heart pure?' You're going to need a pure heart, and it might be just as well to find out *now* whether or not you have one."

Twenty-One

Narmer stalked into his tent and tossed his helmet onto his cot. He flopped into the folding chair behind his worktable. The chair gave out a chorus of squeaks.

Narmer's field dwelling was a standard military tent. He liked that about it. Standard. Military. Nothing special. Granted his tent was connected to the tents housing his servants and his scribes, and granted he didn't share it with a dozen men-at-arms, and granted it was furnished with a combined shrine to Anhur, the Egyptian God of War, and to Mekhit, His consort, and to Amun-Ra, Narmer's father among the Gods; but it remained a military tent. It was cold in winter, stuffy in summer, and it often leaked in the rain.

The two men Narmer had sent for on his way in from the demonstration were waiting outside. He'd passed them on his way into his tent, but he had pointedly ignored their quizzical looks.

The two men's timeliness had been wise on their parts.

Narmer poured himself a glass of beer, sat at his worktable, and called them in.

Harakhty, his envoy to the Mother Metropolitan and the master of Narmer's spies within her court, and Tsekani, his battlemaster, entered, bowed, approached, and stood at attention. They were side by side on the opposite side of the worktable from Narmer.

They held their helmets in the crooks of their left arms. Very military! Wouldn't it be wonderful if they could do their jobs half as well as they could kiss ass?

"You saw?" Narmer asked.

"We did, from a distance," Tsekani said.

"Your opinion?" Narmer asked.

"Flying rocks are flying rocks, no matter what throws them," Tsekani said "We've overcome worse obstacles."

"I commend your optimism," Narmer said.

Why hadn't his subordinates reported one thing of substance to him about Vlod's cannons? Were Harakhty and Tsekani bald-faced failures or were they bungling traitors?

Tsekani said, "The cavalry will sweep down on those hellish machines and destroy them."

This was military fantasy at its worst. The cavalry would be under fire the whole time. Their only hope would be to rush those weapons. In effect, the cavalry would have to close with Vlod's cannons between volleys.

If Narmer were to send in a hundred riders, how many of them would survive the charge? How many would be left to come to grips with the crews serving the cannons?

Tsekani added, "The cavalry will carry the day!"

"Yes, I'm sure they will," Narmer said. "I'm also sure that Edmund will leave his cannons out in the open, unprotected, where my horsemen will be able to attack them with impunity."

Tsekani colored.

The man's embarrassment was overdue.

Tsekani said, "I—"

"Leave me. Both of you," Narmer said. "You're a pair of ignorant fops."

Ashen faced, they bowed and backed out of the tent.

Narmer instructed his guard to admit no one.

With that done, and with the flap to his tent closed, he stretched out on his cot. He had two problems to solve. First, he had two incompetents to make an example of, and second, he had a restive ally to force back into line.

Clear enough.

The first would be the work of a moment.

But the second.

How to accomplish the second?

———

Shortly after Barkley left Ulricka's pavilion, the coffee arrived. She downed half a cup without a pause, and sent for her chef.

When he arrived, she rattled off her instructions for that night's dinner and assured him that although stew and kebabs were an unusual combination, they were in the field and no one would hold it against him. An audacious, adventurous, spicy stew, served hot, would—she had no doubt—be a welcome change from the ordinary run of camp fair. As for the kebabs, well, they would provide a note of variety. They would be easy to eat and a delight to behold. Not only that, but an elegant, costly main dish might be mistaken for pretense.

The chef slobbered his approval. How perceptive Her Beatitude was. How gracious. How generous. How astute. *Tonight?*

"*Astute* is a synonym for *perceptive*," she said.

"Why, yes, Your Beatitude, so it is," the cook said. "My apologies."

"Tonight. Later on. Seven, shall we say?"

"Seven?"

He looked as though she'd asked him to cook without fire.

"Seven."

"Ah, seven o'clock. What an outstanding hour. Inspired. Positively inspired. A triumph, Your Beatitude," he said, and backed out of the room.

The flap closed.

Stew. And Kebabs. Couldn't forget those. Xenia would enjoy that addition. But what else could the kitchen do with that shattered carcass? A fondue? Heaven forbid!

The tent flap flew up, and Shabnan brought in a fresh pot of tea.

Based on the aroma, Ulricka decided it was another one of the Crone's herbal concoctions. No doubt, she'd laced it with a mild sedative.

"You need to lie down," Shabnan said.

That settled it: a sedative.

"I need to speak to Ziellottes," Ulricka said. She poured from a truly ancient silver pot, topping off her coffee. "Send someone to find him and tell him I'd like to speak with him as soon as convenient."

Shabnan put up a fuss, but in the end, she left to detail a runner.

Ulricka leaned to one side in her chair. She propped her head on her fist and closed her eyes.

In his letter, Vlod had captured the truth of their situation: omission was commission. To allow another to violate the Harmony was to violate the Harmony oneself. Of necessity, she would stand condemned before the Goddess. Of necessity, the Goddess would condemn her.

But neither could she permit those weapons to frighten her into submission. She could not allow herself to be intimidated. It would turn the metropolitanate into a plaything for whichever thug commanded the largest army.

"Your Beatitude?"

It was Shabnan.

Ulricka sat up and opened her eyes. "Yes?"

"I've brought Ziellottes."

Had she fallen asleep, or had Ziellottes been near to hand?

Near to hand, surely.

Although her mouth did taste as though she had dozed off.

But in her chair?

It was unthinkable.

She must be closer to the edge than she'd had any idea, staggering between the waking and the dreaming worlds.

The old spy came in and bowed politely. No more than a polite bow. The minimum required by etiquette. The gesture spoke volumes. *I am at your service, but I am not at your command.* How like a magus he was! No surprise there. He was a magus, although he had withdrawn from his guild decades ago.

To Shabnan, Ulricka said, "Please leave us."

"Yes, Your Beatitude."

The flap closed and Ulricka and Ziellottes were alone.

Ulricka pointed across the room. "I have pen, ink, paper, and a writing board in that chest. Would you bring them?"

"My pleasure," Ziellottes said, and began to assemble the items.

Ulricka said, "I've sent Barkley—you know him, don't you?"

"I do," Ziellottes said.

He handed her the items she'd requested.

"Is he one of your spies?" she asked.

"No. I tried to recruit him a few years ago, but he refused. He may be an old charlatan, but he's devoted to you."

"Jinhai claimed to be devoted."

"He was devoted."

"He betrayed me."

"He was devoted to the Cathedral, not to you."

"In betraying me, he betrayed the Cathedral."

"He believed differently."

Ziellottes ended up holding the ink.

Ulricka said, "I ought to have you executed."

"You could, but it would be a shame for you to lose me."

"Would it? Why is that?"

"Because I will never lie to you. I may withhold, I may be mistaken, but I will never lie."

"You're like a character out of a saga."

"Thank you, Your Beatitude."

She scribbled a note, folded it over, wrote *Barkley* across the face. "I sent him out to augur the steer. It won't be a proper augury, of course, but it might prove instructive."

"It might," Ziellottes said, agreeing.

"You ought to have a talk with Barkley. Catch up on old times. That sort of thing." She handed the note to Ziellottes. "You'll find that helpful."

"Thank you."

"Now get out of here before I have you arrested."

Ziellottes bowed, genuinely this time, she thought, and left.

Shabnan entered before the flap had fallen back into place.

"It's time," Shabnan said. "You've done what you can do for the moment. You need to rest." She thrust a steaming cup into Ulricka's hand. "Drink it before it turns cold. When it's cold it tastes like week-old sweat."

"How do you know what week-old sweat tastes like?"

"My squandered youth," Shabnan said.

Ulricka gave herself over. "Very well." Why keep a crone around if not to obey her once in a while?

It was wonderful to relinquish responsibility for a few short hours on a summer afternoon. The tea was hot and sweet.

Drugged.

She had suspected that it would be, and indeed it was.

Within moments, Ulricka hovered in that warm comfort that lurks between wakefulness and sleep. She spiraled down and down, the sky above, the ground below, the cathedral henge all around her.

Was her heart pure?

She believed that it was, but *was* it?

Down.

She could be lying to herself.

Down.

She often did, but she could never quite be sure.

Near the bottom now.

What was the difference between self-deception and hope? Between a comforting lie and faith?

Purity of heart.

Was her heart pure?

What about Jinhai? Could he have told her? Had killing him told her? She was afraid it had.

Down.

Down.

Purity?

Did she have it?

The steer would tell her.

Its entrails would bellow to her.

Was her heart lighter than a feather?

Why couldn't she determine it for herself?

Confusion.

Self-deception.

Her own thumb on the balance.
Ambition.
Fear.
Stupidity.
Naïveté.
The distractions of her office.
Why had she accepted election?
Because Thora had asked her to.
Falling faster now...faster and faster.
The Earth reached up to embrace her...

Twenty-Two

Ziellottes did his best to *stroll* across the field between the armies. He had to appear to be an old man out to visit another old man. It was inconceivable that two old men could pose any threat to the youngsters arrayed on either side.

Such a notion was pure drivel.

Two old men were— Never mind what they were.

Suffice it to say that Ziellottes and Barkley were two of the more dangerous people in the basin. Most-dangerous honors went to Narmer, but for vastly different reasons.

Narmer was merely dangerous, whereas Ziellottes and Barkley were deadly. Narmer was a thug, whereas Ziellottes and Barkley were warrior-sages.

Ziellottes found Barkley crouched over the steer's carcass. His assistant was crouched next to him, holding a basin close. Barkley removed a kidney, or part of one, and put it in the basin.

The assistant transferred it to a shallow pan, which sat on a folding worktable. The pan was made of white steel and had to be well over six hundred years old, a treasure among augurs.

"What do you see, you old imposter?" Ziellottes asked, walking up.

Barkley straightened, and stretched his back. It was the response of a man who appreciated a well-timed intrusion, which this evidently had turned out to be.

"Will you never learn the art of silence?" Barkley asked.

"My joints apologize. How are your sinuses?"

"I count myself among the breathing." To his assistant, Barkley said, "Leave us. Go and have a nice piss. I'll make a senile commotion when I want you."

The man bowed and strode off, shoulders squared, back straight. He reeked of offended pride.

Barkley said, "Fresh out of the Academy and flat stupid."

"He's young beyond our recollection."

"I'll stand by *flat stupid*." Barkley sighed. "He's a good worker, though. Where I am, at the Cathedral, I'm lucky to find anyone."

"The Cathedral can be treacherous."

"True enough, but the nub of the problem is the boredom." Barkley gazed off into the distance. "I'd welcome a good war, if it weren't for all the mess." He looked down at the carcass. "Speaking of which... Well, why have you disturbed my prophetic investigations?"

The steer's body cavity had been probed, the remaining organs, or parts of the remaining organs, shifted. The cannonball had mangled many of them beyond recognition.

Puddles of fluid had formed, but the liquid had already congealed. Because it had, the puddles were useless for primary divination.

"What do you see?" Ziellottes asked.

Barkley pointed into the body cavity. "In there?"

Ziellottes nodded.

"The future."

"What else?"

"The present, the will of the Gods, the ambitions of the ambitious."

"What Ulricka pays you to see?" The question was close to an accusation, but Ziellottes wanted to give his on-again-off-again friend a chance to make his integrity clear, to assert that he had not succumbed to life in the mother metropolitan's court. He might be bored by it, but he had not yet been corrupted by it.

"Ulricka pays me to see what *I* see. Nothing else." Barkley grinned.

"She can see whatever she wants to see, for herself. She doesn't require my services for that."

"What sort of a future is it?"

"The sort that's shrouded in darkness."

Ziellottes held out Ulricka's note. "Let's draw it out into the light, shall we?"

Barkley snatched the note and scanned it. "You've read this?"

Ziellottes had. The note instructed Barkley to answer whatever questions Ziellottes asked about the augury. Barkley was to withhold nothing.

"I took the liberty," Ziellottes said. "It wasn't sealed and she's perfectly aware of my profession."

Barkley flipped the paper over.

Was he checking for traces of wax?

Barkley handed it back.

Yes, he had been.

Barkley's fingers had left smears of blood on the paper. "You'll want to keep that."

"Don't you?"

"No. I'm safe enough," Barkley said.

Ziellottes returned the note to his pocket. "Then I'll hang on to it. I'd be a fool not to."

"Don't you trust me?"

"I don't trust her court," Ziellottes said.

"Very wise. Only dolts and my assistant trust that woman's court."

"What have you found?"

"The old question." Barkley shook his head. "What do the bowels say?" he added in a mock-heroic accent.

"Well, what do they say?"

"I wish I had the head. Any word of what Vlod read?"

"Not yet."

"He augured the blood, didn't he?"

"That's a fair assumption."

Barkley nodded. "He's good at that technique."

"Among the best."

"I had to ask my own question."

Ziellottes suspected otherwise, but he didn't interrupt.

"I see a cancer taking hold," Barkley said. "One of the chieftains or someone close to a chieftain."

"Narmer?"

"Don't sound so hopeful."

"You have to admit it would be a mercy, not for him but for the rest of us."

"That it would, but I can't tell who the lucky fellow is. Maybe a battle-master or an heir. A wife wouldn't be out of the question. A dynastic struggle will ensue: assassination, betrayal, death. The usual run of upscale entertainments."

"What's a catastrophe without multiple tragedies?"

"A bloody waste of time, that's what," Barkley said. "It culminates in a massive war."

"So far you haven't read anything you couldn't have deduced from the way the clans are dancing around one another."

"What about the cancer?"

Ziellottes rolled his eyes. "Given the number of chieftains on hand, it's safe enough to say that one or more of them has it."

"Have you lost your faith entirely?"

"Never mind my faith, what about the war?" Ziellottes asked.

"It will be fought to redress a great evil."

Now there was a revelation if ever there was one!

Despite this flash of cynicism, however, Ziellottes felt a ball of fear spin in his stomach. "Vlod's cannons?"

"No. Narmer's right about their importance, or lack of it. Men-at-arms adjust. No, compared to what's over the horizon, cannons are mere amusements."

"Amusements, you say?"

"The evil *is* great," Barkley said, "but the war will fail to re-cork the bottle. I ought to call the conflict a jihad, because that's what it will be." He waved a blood-smeared hand at the assembled armies. "It'll be completely unlike the present exercise."

The ball in Ziellottes' gut spun faster. "All that from one gut pile?"

"Don't forget the powder burns."

Ziellottes found the entry wound. Black smudges surrounded it. "You mean these marks?"

"No. Those are powder traces."

"Then where are the powder burns?"

"The powder burns are yet to happen, but if this war isn't brought to heel, they will."

"What's a powder burn?" Ziellottes asked.

"Pray you never find out. Pray none of us ever sees them firsthand. Pray the ground swallows those damned machines."

"But they aren't the *great evil*?"

"No, they're not."

"What is?"

"We are."

Ziellottes shivered. It wasn't like him to shiver.

"We are?"

"Our cowardice, I should say."

"The magi?"

"No one else. The chieftains, the Cathedral, the ordinary people— they act on what we tell them, sooner or later," Barkley said. "They believe us! All too often we tell them what they've paid us to tell them. Ulricka calls us whores, and so we are. I call us cheap whores and slavish cowards."

"You're no whore, and you're no coward."

"Am I not?"

"No."

"You know it's true, though, about the magi as a body, and so does Vlod."

"Yes, he knows it better than the guilds and the College combined."

"Better than any of us, except his father."

Vlod's father had been the greatest intellect of his generation, and the cathedral had burned him at the stake before he'd reached forty. The clans, the guilds, and the College had let it happen. They'd kept silent or they'd cheered it on or, in some cases, they'd been complicit. Every stinking one of them had been afraid to be the next to burn.

Ziellottes asked, "What will you tell Ulricka?"

Barkley shrugged. "That her heart is pure."

"You can't be serious! That old shibboleth?"

"What other old shibboleth do you suggest? Shall I tell her that she's acting for the benefit of the people? She knows better than that and so do I."

———

Ulricka had slept far into the afternoon, and woke up feeling as though she were climbing out of a pool of warm quicksand.

Her mouth tasted foul and her face felt greasy.

It ought to feel greasy. It *was* greasy: from field cooking, too many oily foods, from too much coffee, and from not enough face-washing.

It was the same whenever she went hunting for two or three days at a time.

Worse, much worse, however, were the aftereffects of Shabnan's potion.

Ulricka's body was present, the baby was present—and kicking Ulricka's bladder—but Ulricka's mind seemed to have taken a vacation.

Ulricka used the commode, brushed her teeth, washed her hands and face, and did what she could with her hair.

Her mirror showed her face to be the wreck of ages: puffy and blotched. Her skin sagged on her cheekbones, and a huge pimple had broken out on her forehead. The miserable thing was off to one side, so maybe she could cover it with a lock of hair or a hat.

She ought to have outgrown blemishes years ago, and she still might if she lived long enough. The one compensation of menopause might be the end of such eyesores, but long before it was she'd be dead.

She changed into a lightweight gown and put on sandals instead of boots. She was through with riding for the day.

Shabnan carried in a coffee service. Next to the pot was a stack of sweet cakes. Fat and grease. Ulricka told herself that she ought to ignore them, but she had the rest of the afternoon and the evening to get through. She had to be alert. And, like it or not, the sugar and the wheat would help.

"I was about to wake you," Shabnan said brightly.

Ulricka was in no mood for Shabnan's motherly cheerfulness. "Don't ever presume to do that again," she said, and lowered herself into a chair.

Shabnan set the service on the sideboard. "Do what?" she asked, and poured a cup of coffee. She handed it to Ulricka. "Sweet cake?"

"You slipped me a double draft," Ulricka said.

"You could have spit it out."

"You would have pried my jaws open and poured it down my throat."

"You needed to sleep."

"I need a clear head."

"Indeed you do," Shabnan said. She put two sweet cakes on a plate and set it within Ulricka's reach. "Which is why you needed to sleep."

Ulricka spooned honey into her coffee and swirled it around until it dissolved. Coffee was one of Shabnan's talents, and Ulricka drank it off in one long, glorious swallow. The brew might just kick her mind into life, dispel the adolescent churlishness.

"Is Narmer camped out on my doorstep?" Ulricka asked.

Shabnan's eyes widened. "How did you know?" she asked.

"He lacks creativity."

"He has his battlemaster with him."

"Ah, I see I'm to be chastised."

"Over my dead body. Chastising you is my job."

<hr>

Ulricka received Narmer and Tsekani in the sitting room of her pavilion. A breeze gusted in through the widows. The fresh air diluted the odors of armor, metal polish, horse dung, and sweat that the two men exuded.

Shabnan stood behind and to the right of Ulricka's chair.

Narmer said, "You can't back down. It would destroy your credibility."

"What about Edmund's new weapons?" Ulricka asked.

"Soldiers are destined to die in battle," Narmer said.

"The first volley may frighten them," Tsekani said, "but after that, they'll settle down and do their duty."

He was so quick with that assertion that it had to have been memorized.

"What would you have me do?" Ulricka asked.

"Attack. We have the upper hand."

"I agree," Tsekani said.

"Yes, of course you do," Shabnan said. "You wouldn't dare not agree." She smirked. "I've seen Harakhty's head, up there on its pike. Whoever lopped it off has no great martial skill. Sloppy work. Needlessly cruel."

Narmer's eyes narrowed.

Was his anger the earnest of a blood feud? Ulricka was convinced that it was. Then again, so what? He'd had the Cathedral in his sights for years. He had been born coveting it.

How had she ever imagined that she could neuter him with a few promises of greater influence and fairer treatment?

Ulricka said, "We shall take no military action until tomorrow, if then. Tonight we'll have a civilized dinner and discuss our options like civilized adults. You will participate fully and honestly. Am I understood?"

Twenty-Three

The late afternoon sun warmed Vlod's face.

The Mother Metropolitan's dinner, now being called a banquet, was due to begin in a couple of hours, but in the meantime, the opposing armies had permitted themselves to relax, to stand back, if not stand down.

Out among his cannons, Vlod sat on the ground, his back to a wagon wheel. The spokes were large enough not to be uncomfortable. The ground was dry, and the grass was fragrant. Not a hint of rain, but the breeze was coming up, or behaving as though it might be.

Brenna's energetic stomp approached from the direction of the main gate.

Vlod locked his eyelids closed.

He felt her shadow fall over him. She jostled his leg with the toe of her boot. "Open your eyes, magus. Why did you defy my father?"

"That was this morning," Vlod said.

"And this is this afternoon."

"You should have come sooner. I'm fresh out of answers."

Brenna tapped Vlod's leg. Any harder and it would have been a blow. "Out with it!"

Vlod opened one eye and peered up at her. "Kick me again and I'll turn you into a frog."

"You couldn't turn a tadpole into a frog."

"Would you rather be a toad?"

"I'd rather you answered my question."

Vlod closed his eyes, but he tensed one set of muscles and relaxed another. If she tried to use him for a soccer ball a third time, it would not go well for her. "Don't you need to change into court dress?"

"I didn't bring court dress, as you call it. Answer the question."

"Ask your father."

Her foot left the grass as she cocked it for another kick.

Vlod rolled toward her. He struck with his legs and pulled on the hem of her uniform tunic. She toppled over with a shriek and sprawled on the ground. She scrambled to gain room, but he refused to let her disengage.

After a brief, intense struggle, she ended up on her back. He was sitting astride her and had her arms pinned to the ground.

It was like old times on the beach...or like current times when they were up to no good.

"Are you going to the banquet or not?" he asked.

"Yes. Are you?"

"I'm the guest of *dis*honor," he said.

He eased away from her. He expected a revenge attack, but when none came, he offered her his hand. Using it, she pulled herself up. They sat face-to-face on the grass.

"Why didn't you obey him?" she asked.

Vlod glanced out across the field. "It was a beautiful morning. It would have been a shame to spend it killing people."

She gaped at him. "Why warn them?"

"We're alive. Reason enough, wouldn't you say?"

"Narmer would have attacked right onto your weapons. We would have won!"

"War isn't a perishable commodity."

"Very funny."

"But also very true."

She scoffed. "What about the augury? What did the steer's head tell you? Whatever it was, Father's been in a better mood since you told him."

"I examined the head, read its blood, to the extent that I could. Congealed blood—"

"Skip the lecture. What did it tell you?"

"It didn't have much to say. Steers rarely do. No balls."

She grimaced. "What about the augury?"

"It was a load of nonspecific rubbish."

"What did you tell him?"

"That the situation was fluid, that he had unlimited scope for maneuver," Vlod said. "It's one of the standard pronouncements when the reading turns up blank. Officially, the Gods and the Generations have declined to speak; therefore, They are bestowing an unlimited scope of choices."

"I don't like this side of you."

"Maybe I ought to have told him his heart is pure."

"Is that what Barkley will have told Ulricka?"

"If he has a brain in his head."

Brenna considered. "Augurs lie?"

"I don't, but it happens. Anyway, her heart is pure, by her own lights. Your father does have an unlimited number of things he can do at this point. No lying required." Vlod got to his feet. "I have to dress for the banquet—change into clothes that don't smell like horseshit."

"Will you take a bath?" she asked.

Vlod smiled. "I'll share if you'd like."

"I would," Brenna said, and held out her hand to him.

He took it and pulled her to her feet.

"I'm glad we're still alive," he said.

"So am I."

TWENTY-FOUR

The Mother Metropolitan held her banquet under an expansive awning that her staff had cobbled together from tents and sails. They and countless men-at-arms had also torn apart several supply wagons and used the planks to knock together tables and benches.

The whole of it, from the tent poles to the table legs, was crude and rickety, barely standing. It served as an additional proof that although one woman can produce a baby in nine months, nine women cannot produce a baby in one month. But it would serve.

Ulricka—or Shabnan acting for her—had invited major and minor chieftains, their battlemasters, their senior retainers, and select members of their immediate families. It wasn't a large group, but it was larger than Vlod had expected for what had been announced as a working meal, a working banquet.

The head table was an expanse of snowy linen. Smaller pieces had been overlain to make the whole. The china and crystal glittered; the cutlery gleamed. There were mismatches, to be sure, but they added a welcoming note of impromptu, spontaneous elegance.

Edmund, Brenna, and Wolfram, together with Ulricka, Shabnan, Xenia, Vernon, Narmer, Seldon, and their assorted battlemasters basked in the extemporized luxury.

The tables at which Ulricka's staff had seated Vlod and Dagna were expanses of not-so-snowy cotton and not-so-gleaming plates and utensils: pottery rather than china, glass rather than crystal, polished iron rather than silver.

Ulricka was hugely pregnant, but her color was good and she conversed in an animated manner. Shabnan was gray, her eyes dark-circled. She was acting middle-aged.

Dagna sat not far from Gregory, and they acted out their mutual indifference with panache.

Brenna—bless her!—was in uniform, including her best sword and battle knife. She looked as though she had fitted herself out for a formal-dress battle to the death but had wound up at a peace negotiation.

Ulricka, Narmer, Seldon, Edmund, and Vernon were a grim bunch, despite their effusive laughter.

The minor chieftains were too busy with the food and the serving girls to pick fights among themselves. They had been ordered to be polite, and polite they were.

About the time the food was cool enough to eat, one by one, those seated at the head table rose and made their exits.

A quarter of an hour later, a messenger brought Vlod a note.

It was from Edmund, and instructed Vlod to join the negotiations.

Vlod entered the sitting room of Ulricka's pavilion. A blast of humid summer air enveloped him. A scant three meters on a side, the room was enormous for a pavilion, but it was inadequate for the number of people packed into it.

Vlod's skin prickled, and he began to sweat. The different perfumes the women were wearing clashed, and someone's boots weren't as clean as they ought to have been. Grass and shit were never a good mix indoors.

Those present were seated around a large table, the sides mixed. This wasn't about opposition. It was about reaching an accord.

At Edmund's instruction, Vlod sat next to him. Wolfram was on the opposite side of the table, directly across.

"You're here to answer a few questions," Edmund said. "Answer fully, but we want information, not lectures."

"Yes, my lord," Vlod said. He felt like a schoolboy.

Shabnan asked, "Magus, how can we eradicate the cannons you've built?"

"Eradicate? I'm not sure what you mean."

"Destroy."

"Load them, plug the tubes with cement, let it harden, and then touch them off from a safe distance. The detonations will blow them apart."

Wolfram arched a warning eyebrow.

Vlod hastily added, "Less dramatically, you could disassemble them."

"This is absurd," Narmer said. "His work—"

"Please," Shabnan said. To Vlod, she said, "You misunderstand, in part. I must have stated it badly. Allow me to try a second time. Yes, how can we destroy the cannons you've built, but more to the point, how can we ensure that cannons remain in the past?"

"How can you disinvent them?" Vlod asked.

"Exactly."

"You can't," Vlod said.

"Why not?"

"Because you have no way to enforce your prohibition without recourse to the very weapons you seek to prohibit."

"You underestimate us," Ulricka said.

"No, my father underestimated you," Vlod said. "I do not."

A gasp rippled around the chamber.

"In a way, innovation is like the Black Death, like smallpox, like a host of other plagues," Vlod said. "To prevent contagion, you must burn out the source of the infection."

"What about the libraries?" Ulricka asked. "That's where you learned how to build them, wasn't it?"

"Only in part," Vlod said, and left the rest unsaid, the part about intelligence, work, experimentation, and courage.

"Yes, I understand—"

Like hell she did.

"—but couldn't we purge the libraries of all references to cannons and the like? Wouldn't that discourage this nonsense?"

"No, just the opposite," Vlod said. "In order to prohibit a technology you must first know what it is you're trying to prohibit. You must know what it does, how it works, and how it's built; otherwise, how do you know, day to day, what to prohibit and what to allow? You have to have a meter stick."

"Nonsense," Ulricka said.

"Tell me, Your Beatitude, are you also prepared to ban gunpowder, metal pipe, carpentry, forging, casting, and scores of other disciplines, let alone curiosity and raw intelligence? If you don't, sooner or later, someone else is sure to combine the necessary elements and produce cannons. Cannons lurk, unseen, and, often, unsuspected, within the routine technologies we depend upon."

"Without your example it may never occur to them," Shabnan said.

"You underestimate the inventiveness of desperate, or greedy, human beings."

Narmer said, "I am not—"

Cutting him off, Shabnan asked, "Perhaps, but your example only exacerbates the problem."

"My apologies."

"Don't get smart with me," Shabnan snapped. Without waiting for a response, she asked, "Under what conditions would you be willing to destroy your work?"

"Why negotiate?" Narmer demanded. "The man's a heretic. Those who've supported him are heretics! They deserve to be expunged from the face of the earth!"

To Vlod, Ulricka calmly said, "Please answer the question."

With a detachment he did not feel, Vlod said, "I am Edmund's loyal subject."

"The magi do not have lords!" Narmer shouted.

It was one of the older maxims, a distillation of centuries of practice, of hundreds of rules intended to enshrine the impartiality, the neutrality, the independence of the magi. In theory, it ensured their survival. As a body, they were rather like the Cathedral in that regard.

The moment a magus graduated from one or another of the academies, he ceased to be a member of his clan and was henceforth prohibited from clan membership. The College of Magi inducted him and he joined one or another of the recognized guilds.

His guild, in turn, assigned him to a local chapter.

In terms of the formalities, it was the local chapters that served the particular clans, and it was the local chapters that, under normal circumstances, assigned their members to specific tasks within the clan.

The magi *served* their assigned clans and chieftains, but the clans and chieftains were not at liberty to *command* them.

A magus's first loyalty was to the College of Magi, his second was to his guild, and his third was to his chapter. The College forbade any acknowledgement of a fourth claim. For a magus to profess one would be an act of self-condemnation.

As a consequence, the magi did not have lords.

Vlod, however, was the anomaly. He was the quiet exception to which the College, the guilds, and the chapters turned a blind eye.

Vlod decided that it was time for him to make a measure of noise.

He said, "I was born among the Iredales, I work among the Iredales, and I shall die among the Iredales. I *am* an Iredale. The disposition of any work I perform is for my lord Edmund to decide. The work is not mine."

A gasp rippled through the chamber.

Before Narmer could resume his tirade, Edmund said, "Our demands don't amount to much."

His tone was so unlike him, so conciliatory, that it took Vlod aback. Was this the feint before the final lunge?

"What are they?" Shabnan asked.

She tried to match Edmund's tone, but missed it. Rather than sounding as if she were willing to reach an agreement, she had sounded like the jaws of a trap being pried open, like the pan locking into place. Now all that was left for her to do was to wait for him to step onto it and spring the jaws.

Edmund said, "We'll dispose of Vlod's work in exchange for the Mother Metropolitan's approval of Dagna and Gregory's marriage."

"We're back to that damn alliance," Seldon said.

"You're abnormally perceptive for a silk merchant," Vernon said.

Seldon jumped to his feet, his hand on his sword, but Xenia motioned for him to sit down. "Let's hear Edmund out," she said. "If you start a fight now, you'll always wonder about the details of what else he has to propose."

Seldon dropped back into his chair.

Turning to Edmund, Xenia said, "You do have a *what else* prepared, don't you?"

"Indeed I do," Edmund said. "I will also cooperate in the formation and operation of a commission to *advise* me on the operation of the river bar and its upriver and ocean approaches. In return—"

"Let's cut through the rhetoric, shall we?" Ulricka said.

"Fine by me," Edmund said.

"You'll trade the cannons for the marriage?"

"Yes."

"*And* you'll allow a commission to advise you on the operation of the channels, the port, and the river bar?"

"Not the port. The port's mine. So are the river and bar pilots. The port and the pilots are off limits. Absolutely off limits."

"Very well," Ulricka said.

"Who'll nominate the members of the commission?" Edmund asked.

"How about the council of chieftains?" Shabnan suggested.

"Very well, but the nominees must have my approval. I won't tolerate a committee of Narmer's lackeys."

Ulricka's anger flashed. "Nor can I permit a commission made up of your toadies."

How little that woman understood!

Edmund arched an eyebrow. "I don't have toadies."

"You don't? I thought everyone did," Ulricka said. A brittle silence settled over the meeting. She broke it. "Very well. You have your right of approval."

"And you must leave Vernon and me to work out our own successions."

"The Cathedral does not meddle—" Shabnan said.

"Done," Ulricka said.

Narmer said, "You have no right to conclude an agreement without our allies' consent."

"I fully intend to consult *my* allies."

"They're not yours; they're *mine*."

Ulricka drew herself up. The strain of her pregnancy showed in the tightness around her eyes.

"You may go," she said. "I have not forgotten the captain of *The Wings of Nekhbet*."

"How many men-at-arms do you command?"

"Men-at-arms, is it?" Ulricka asked. "I am the living avatar of the Great Goddess! I have the power to call down the forces of Heaven and Earth! You are dismissed."

Narmer stormed into his tent. "Get Reshef in here on the double!" he bellowed. He threw himself into the chair behind his worktable. In a fit of temper, he swept the surface clean with his arm. Papers flew and the inkwell splashed. The lamp spun in the air like an acrobat and clattered onto the floor. The tumble was so violent that, impossibly, the oil drowned the lamp's flames rather than being ignited by them.

A serving girl rushed in, but Narmer sent her right back out. It was his mess, and he'd clean it up.

When it came to his other mess, he wished to heaven that he *could* clean it up, but that was impossible.

Narmer set the lamp on his desk. The reservoir had retained a dribble of oil. He relit the lamp's three wicks.

He sat down behind his worktable and began to sort his papers into their original stacks.

Reshef, the head of his special-orders group, the Sekhmet Battalion, entered. "My lord?" he asked. "How may I serve?"

Narmer looked up from the pages. "It's time we introduced Her Beatitude to the Fangs of Wadjet."

TWENTY-FIVE

The negotiations had reconvened the next morning. The parties had stacks of details left to hash out, a myriad of procedures to agree on, and countless terms to clarify.

They made a good start, but as the morning ground on, progress slowed to an agonizing trickle.

With the sun past its zenith, Ulricka declared their work concluded—" for the present"—and dismissed them.

They'd left the bulk of their work undone, but exactitude, she had decided, would have to be the province of later sessions, sessions that would take place away from restive armies that had come to do battle but were instead digging latrines and washing dishes and performing endless, noisy drills.

In the meantime, until those future negotiations had been completed, the parties had no choice but to rely on self-interest to carry them through. Sooner or later, practices and accommodations *on the ground* would solidify into something like a working arrangement.

In the meantime, their secretaries and scribes, their underlings and military personnel would be scribbling for days on end before they had the initial understandings down, black ink on white paper.

At this juncture, Ulricka sensed, it would be no inept thing to send the armies home, home before they could invent an excuse on their own to fight the battle that had been denied them.

Outside the Mother Metropolitan's pavilion, Vlod made his excuses to Edmund and Wolfram, and went off on his own.

He needed time to consider what had happened over the past few days and to think through what might happen next.

In exposing himself with such defiance, in demonstrating the power of his cannon, in declaring himself loyal to Edmund, rather than to the College of Magi, he had exposed both Edmund and Clan Iredale, but he had had no choice in any of it.

Both the demonstration and his declaration had been utterly necessary.

Edmund would never trust him again, of course, not in the old way, and Ulricka would never forgive him, for being Edmund's man, for choosing the Iredales over the College.

Within days, within hours, he would find himself subtly but forcefully excluded.

He would be lucky to live out the year.

But Brenna would!

And that was enough.

Upon reaching the eastern edge of the encampment, Vlod scrambled up the side of an ancient flood-control dike. Because trees, brush, and grass had overgrown it, to the casual eye it appeared to be a natural feature and not a human construction.

He paused at the top and looked out over the river.

The two fleets rode at anchor, bow to bow. On the downstream hand, Edmund's fleet had anchored bow to current; while directly in front of Vlod, Narmer's and Ulricka's ships had anchored stern to current.

The Mother Metropolitan could not allow Vlod's actions and declarations to go unanswered, but neither could Narmer allow Ulricka's drubbing of him go unrevenged. But how would Narmer, the would-be Pharaoh respond?

He had dozens of options: social snubbing, withdrawal from their alliance, assassination, the outright conquest of the Cathedral, the building of public temples to the Egyptian Gods and Goddesses, and so on.

Which would he choose?

The question made for an interesting puzzle.

Vlod picked his way down to the sand at the water's edge. Wavelets curled and broke across the grains, which were coarse and mixed with small rocks and twigs.

A tree had stranded between the beach and the dirt bank. The tree was whole, with the trunk and roots at one end and the branches and leaves, now dried and brown and cracking, at the other. The previous spring freshet had deposited it. Or perhaps not. Whatever the case, it offered an inviting place to rest.

Vlod sat down on the trunk and watched the water.

With Ulricka handed over to her attendants, Shabnan was free to do as she pleased with the rest of the afternoon. She pleased to make herself a pot of herb tea and to sit in her broom closet of a room in the pavilion and read a book.

The tea was no less vile than Ulricka claimed it was, and Shabnan was unable to drink it without accidently sloshing it over the rim of her cup.

Why did her hands tremble like frightened rabbits, and why had the tea upset her stomach?

The words blurred on the page of her book.

She changed her mind.

Rather than sit in her room, it pleased her to go for a walk. She yearned to lay herself out on the sacrificial altar at the cathedral, to indulge herself in a fit of irreverent piety, to have sex with one of the priests—Such hot-blooded boys!—but the cathedral was out of reach.

The air was soft, and the camp had quieted down. From horses to military commanders, everyone was munching, gossiping, smoking, or drinking. Horses didn't smoke or gossip, but they were engaged in the equine equivalents. The hot-grease smell of cooking hung between the tents.

How that fool had gone on! The future pharaoh, the Man-God of the basin—he was no better than a pile of maggot-infested excrement! Did he believe—

Shabnan let out a ragged sigh. Her outrage was useless. She refocused her attention on the world around her.

The sun had dropped close to the line of hills to the west. Soon the mosquitoes would come out to play, and the swallows would swoop and dive, chasing after them. The bats, too.

People nodded to her, and she was scrupulous to return their greetings.

Each exchange, each smile, each wave, each nod, as pleasant as they were, increased her sense of dread, of imprisonment, of the inexorable approach of old age, infirmity, and death.

She walked faster and faster.

The faces blurred, and the greetings went unreturned.

She ran up a short rise, reached the top, and stared down at the river. It was a placid, unconcerned ribbon of blue-gray.

Eternal.

Until it wasn't anymore.

Even rivers and mountains died.

Her legs felt as if they were about to collapse out from under her, collapse like rotten pilings.

Rot.

The word *was* apt.

If the passing years didn't bring rot, what did they bring?

Not youth.

Wisdom? Perspective?

Maybe, but a hell of a lot of good those would do her in the grave. It was better to be young and stupid and fertile than to be old and wise and dried up.

What manner of hell must Ricki be going through these days!

Shabnan stood at the top of the rise. Her chest heaved, and her lungs burned. A muck sweat drenched her body and an evil chill rattled her. She pressed her eyes closed.

She hugged herself and rocked back and forth.

Then she stood still.

She relaxed her chest and abdominal muscles. She timed her breaths with a slow count, as though she were performing an asana. Ten count in, ten count out; over and over, ride the rhythm, join with the Prana. Send the breath deep. Exhale from the very base of the spine, from the Muladhara chakra. Send the breath out through the top of the skull, out through the Sahasrara chakra. Energize the chakras and calm the body, silence the monkey mind, nourish the soul.

Again and again.

Do not be afraid.

Not a command, but a reassurance.

Dance with Shiva.

Become one with Shiva Nataraja, Lord of the Dance.

The breath, in and out.

Ride the Prana.

Ride the dance.

Ride the breath.

Ride the flow of time.

The crisis eased, and she opened her eyes.

The river stretched out before her. On the opposite shore lay Vernon's lands, the Land of the Six Rivers. They were green with trees, burgeoning with life.

Closer to her, a strip of sand bordered the bottom of the rise on which she stood. The rise had to be the remains of an ancient...of an ancient *something*. She couldn't say what. Towpath? Dike? Dam? Defensive wall?

The beach was empty except for one lone figure a few meters downstream. The figure was a man. He was sitting on an uprooted tree. Small in stature. He was not in uniform but carried an array of weapons: a long sword, a battle knife, and at least two throwing knives. He was Vlod, Edmund's pet magus.

Did the surfeit of weapons mean that he was afraid?

He had good cause to be.

Ricki persisted in her desire to toast him, and Narmer would like nothing nearly as much as killing him.

Like a dog that's being stared at, the runt looked up. He shaded his eyes, and waved to her, a friendly wave.

She waved in return, but then she turned away and walked upstream.

She saw the hint of what might have been a roadway, or perhaps it had been a towpath. In truth, it could have been anything from a deliberate construction to a deposit the river had built up.

———

Vlod watched the Crone's departure for a time, but he soon returned his focus to the river. There was a lot to see and watching it relaxed him. Next to the water itself, the herons were without equal. They were massive blue-gray birds, patient beyond belief. And, at that very moment, in slow, cautious movements, a Great Blue hunted in the shallows.

Birds...

In the millennia before the Second Creation, augury had originated as a method of divining the will of the Gods by reading the flight of birds. Either observed in nature or caged and released on command, a bird or birds would fly or perch or strut. Through various means, an augur would read the behavior and derive the divination.

Following the Second Creation, the term *augury* had come to encompass a broad complex of techniques. Dice, cards, animal and human entrails, blood, and so on took their places next to the behavior of birds. Spirit journeys, spirit canoes, gazing into flames, the inhalation of sacred fumes, the visions sparked by snake venom, and the ecstatic state induced by ritual, among others, also played their roles.

The Guild of Augurs employed a bewildering variety of methods.

However, throughout the changes, the core of augury remained: the reading of the behavior of birds.

At the Academy, during the time that Vlod had attended, Qadir, the augury instructor, had led his charges through year after year of "scholarly memorization." They learned the bones, organs, tendons, and muscles of scores of species. Qadir placed special emphasis on human beings, bald eagles, herons, cormorants, vultures, pigeons, elk, and, for reasons lost to history, sea lions and harbor seals.

The lessons often turned healthy brains into figurative lumps of goo. Eyes clouded over, jaws went slack, ears went deaf, and tongues went numb.

At such times, Qadir would call a halt and regale his charges with stories of the great auguries of the past. His tales often involved the use of birds. Without any of his students realizing it until years afterward, his stories had taught them the practice and the power of augury.

As for the rote, what saved them was that most species, bird to bird, pinniped to pinniped, had nearly identical skeletal structures. The shapes changed, but the placements, and thus the names, remained relatively consistent.

As Shabnan walked upstream, she discovered that she delighted in the spongy give of the ground beneath her feet. The soil crawled with life, a complete change from the dry lands, even close to the river, that surrounded the Cathedral and Maryhill.

It was the rainfall. Had to be. The abundance of water gave rise to different varieties, lush varieties, of flora and fauna.

It bred a different variety of clansman, too.

The people over here were hard but generous, courageous but not reckless. They were insightful and intelligent, but neither sophisticated nor clever. They had no patience with adornment for adornment's sake. For them, their lives and their possessions required practical purpose in the here and now.

This made them an inexpressible threat.

Edmund's runt headed the list of exemplars.

Why, then, had she acknowledged him? Vlod hadn't noticed her until she had inadvertently attracted his attention. Why had they exchanged greetings?

She couldn't speak for him, but she had waved to him out of the common feeling that one human being has for another. His clan and the Cathedral had avoided a conflagration that would have been a wellspring of heresy and death for generations to come. Common feeling, common cause. An unspoken alliance against Narmer united them.

She pulled her clothes—flimsy, summer things—more tightly around her.

A well-worn trail, bordered by short grass, ran along the top of the dike. Dike. She'd choose to call it that for now. The people stationed at Morven's Gate must patrol the area, and they must also turn their cattle out to graze on the bottomland and the dike. Goats, too, by the look of the droppings.

The red-orange wash of the approaching sunset crept into the light.

Already?

Where had the afternoon gone?

Her muck sweat had dissipated, but the tightness in her gut remained.

Suddenly another emotion assailed her, throwing her off balance.

She tried to describe it, to name it.

Fear?

Close, but mild.

Terror?

Better, but extravagant.

She angled down onto the sand and continued upstream.

The cause, the object?

Shabnan proposed and discarded names, situations, and conditions.

The prospect of genuine old age and death? Why were those two never far from her mind these days? Because, you silly old fool, they're very near.

And then a name presented itself. It was the name of a person.

Dumbfounded, she couldn't credit it, but it refused to give place.

Ulricka!

Shabnan's vision darkened, and a sharp pain ripped across her chest. She thought she was going to faint, but she kept her feet.

Ulricka? Could it be?

Yes, it could.

Ulricka!

Ulricka's moods and tempers stretched across the whole disappointing range of human frailty, but Shabnan had never before seen the Mother Metropolitan as she was now: both raging demon and avenging Goddess.

A warm gust of wind buffeted Shabnan's skirts.

A bone-deep chill wracked her.

The emotion that she hadn't been able to name up to now was...*awe*.

Ulricka—self-indulgent, fallible, undisciplined Ulricka—truly was an avatar of the Great Goddess!

The Great Goddess had chosen her to stand in Her place—not symbolically, not spiritually, not mystically, not sentimentally, not figuratively, not sacramentally, but *ontologically*.

Factually.

As factual as the existence of air, earth, fire, and water.

Could such a thing be? Could that spoiled brat, that child in a woman's body, be a personal manifestation—an incarnation!—of the Goddess?

Could she be not merely Her representative, but Her living avatar?

Yes, Ulricka could be.

The wind tore Shabnan's hair from its pins and lashed it across her face.

Yes, not only could she be, she *was*!

Tears filled Shabnan's eyes. They overflowed and ran down.

The sun slipped behind the hills to the west and the darkness began to gather around her. It filled the hollows and leached the color from the land.

Her usefulness to Ulricka was at an end!

Vlod picked up a stone and tossed it into the water.

A nearby heron swiveled its long-beaked head around but otherwise took no notice of him. The bird was too tame for his own good. He reminded Vlod of many of the magi. He reminded Vlod of Vlod.

The augurs Qadir idolized had been heroes, not underlings.

Baker the Muddy—to name one—had been anything but tame. His contemporaries had called him "the muddy" because he often slogged out onto the tide flats and along the riverbanks in order to observe herons and cranes at close quarters.

He loved birds, and he took notes on what he saw, volumes and volumes of notes. They were safely locked away in the library of the

Academy of Archmagus Basil the Anchorite and Wonderworker. How those notes had escaped destruction at the hands of his chieftain, Manthion the Confessor, was a tale worth a book in itself.

Vlod scrunched the toe of his boot into the sand.

The crews of the ships lounged on deck, and the smoke from their galley fires came ashore on the wind. The breeze came from downstream and worked against the current, kicking up a mild chop.

Qadir's version of the story stated that Baker the Muddy conducted his most notorious augury, which involved a Great Blue Heron, on behalf of Petra, Manthion's wife. She was pregnant. Nothing unusual there. She was so fertile that if Manthion smiled at her, she missed her very next period. The worry on the court's mind was that she had convinced herself that although she loved the baby she was carrying, she would—

From his place in the shallows, the heron again captured Vlod's attention. The bird was stalking. A fish? A frog? Every few seconds, he would adopt a new stance, one that was nearer to his prey.

So far so good.

But the bird held his wings in an uncharacteristic position. Herons held their wings against their bodies when they hunted, but this bird was holding them away from his body. Apparently, he couldn't decide whether to take flight or to hunt, and had adopted both postures, that of the hunter and that of the hunted.

Or, to turn the phrase around, the hunted and the hunter.

Vlod's realization of what he was seeing, of what he was *reading*, took hold of him.

As it did, a cold, overpowering sense of urgency swept through him.

He jumped to his feet and dashed toward the encampment.

TWENTY-SIX

Vlod's throwing dagger plucked the cobra from the air.

The two-meter-long snake hit the floor in a writhing, hissing tangle at Ulricka's feet.

She recoiled and screamed, but instantly regained her self-control.

Her hands shaking, she stumbled back to the couch and dropped onto it. Her face was as pale as bone, and her eyes were huge.

"It's not dead yet," Vlod said.

Ulricka drew her legs up.

Four of her guards rushed into the room, weapons drawn. Seconds earlier, Vlod had dashed past them, heedless of their commands.

Pointing at the twisting snake, Vlod said, "Cobra!"

The guards hesitated.

The snake appeared to be tying itself in knots around Vlod knife.

One of the guards pointed her sword at the snake and edged toward it.

"I wouldn't," Vlod said.

The other three guards surrounded Vlod. They didn't dare strike, but neither did they dare assume he wasn't a danger to their mistress.

Ulricka waved them off. "I'd be dead if it weren't for him. Leave us."

They bowed themselves out.

The snake died.

Vlod lifted it from the floor. It was heavy and sleek, an instrument of death.

"Not one of yours?" he asked.

Ulricka shook her head. "No. We left the snakes at the cathedral." Her eyes hardened. "Why did you kill it? You'd be better off if I were dead."

Vlod had to chuckle. The question was trite from overuse in the sagas, but in this case it fit. "Edmund needs you and you need him. I live for the day when the two of you wake up to that fact."

"Was it Edmund who sent it?"

"The Iredales dislike snakes," Vlod said. He handed the carcass out through the door. A horrified guard took it. "Bury it," Vlod said.

Ulricka asked, "Who, then?"

A jumble of pieces fell into place. "Who else keeps cobras? Who might have brought one along? Who is determined to decorate his brow with one?"

"Not Xenia, then? She could be raising snakes."

"Yes, she could, but it's too soon for her to make her move."

"Narmer." Ulricka pronounced the name with the finality of an axe striking.

"We have no evidence."

"We haven't looked," she said.

"You have the makings of a magus," Vlod said. "Your visitor didn't slither in here by accident."

"My guards?"

"Not necessarily. Snakes and their handlers are a stealthy bunch. That said, I'd begin with your guards." He added, "Ziellottes might be willing to lend a hand."

"We have people," Ulricka said.

She went over to her side table, lifted a decanter of amber liquid. "Sherry? It's from the Cathedral's winery."

"Please."

"Depending on the grapes, the batches improve a little every year." She poured two glasses and handed one to Vlod. "A great deal depends on things no one can control."

"So say we all," Vlod said, not sarcastically but in complete agreement.

Ulricka sipped her sherry and smiled. "This batch turned out. Very nice."

Vlod drank a little of his. He was no expert, but it had what he would have described as a clear taste, not in the least harsh. "It's quite good," he said, and took another drink.

"The scribblers are scribbling, but we have business, I believe."

"We do, I think."

"As agreed, I'll approve the marriage, but Edmund will have to cooperate with the commission—cooperate, not ignore. I can't allow him to turn it into window dressing."

"What about Vernon? You'll have to include him. Edmund can't permit himself to be singled out. For now, yes, but not in the long run."

"Vernon worries me less than Edmund does."

"Nevertheless, he must share the burden."

"Very well. He's the Lord of the Six Rivers. Let his navigable waterways come under the commission's purview as well."

"Good." Vlod sipped the sherry. It warmed his mouth and throat in a gentle, civilized manner. "What else?"

"Desmond lives."

"He doesn't deserve to live."

"He lives."

She'd said it with a finality that would brook no dissent.

Vlod dissented. "Not if he shows his face on Iredale land."

"Why is that?"

"First, he's one of your spies. Second, he murdered my foreman, a man named Eakan."

"Not on my orders, he didn't."

"No, not on your orders," Vlod said. "He shares Narmer's penchant for negligent zeal."

"Fair enough," Ulricka said. "I owe you my life." She grimaced. "How banal that sounds." In a mock rescued-damsel voice, she repeated, "I owe you my life." She batted her eyes like a child playing grownup.

He made a dismissive gesture, but he didn't play along. To have taken a share in her self-deprecation would have been to overstep.

She stood. "You'll have to give up your new toys."

"As agreed."

"No, I mean you'll have to *give them up*. Deep down where it counts. No backdoor development. No cherished ambitions. No weaseling."

"No one else builds them, either."

"Absolutely no one else. If anyone tries, I'll find out, and I'll put a stop to it."

Vlod shuddered to imagine what form the stopping would take. Doubtless it would involve stakes, bundles of wood, buckets of pitch, and a flaming torch or two.

"You're on the short end of our exchange."

"Meaning what?" Vlod asked.

"Fair's fair. You've done a lot of giving, and I've done a lot of taking. I need to balance the scales," she said. She went over to her worktable and arranged pen, ink, and paper. She wrote on a sheet of the best imported cotton-rag paper, folded it, and handed it to him. "That should help."

"Thank you," Vlod said, and began to unfold the sheet.

"Not now. Open it when you're alone."

———————

In his tent, Vlod turned up the lantern and unfolded the sheet of paper Ulricka had given him.

To the Mother Superior of the Manor Henge of Desdemona the Shipbreaker, Greetings and Fervent Joy in the Love of the Great Goddess!

Our Dearest and Beloved Mother Charlotte,

Please add Shivananda the Magus to The Dirge Common *to Clan Iredale. Also, please ensure that this addition is reported to the cathedral for inclusion in* The Dirge Common *to the Cathedral Henge of Eileen the Immortal.*

Thank you, and we look forward to our next meeting.

*May the Blessings and Love of the Great Goddess be Upon You and Upon
All Those in Your Devoted Care,*

Ulricka, MM

Vlod refolded the sheet and returned it to the secure pocket inside his
cloak.

It took him three attempts to button the flap.

Narmer had neglected to light a lamp as the evening had darkened, and
now his tent had grown dim, a world of deep shadows and vaguer shapes.
One of those shapes was Reshef, his doer of deeds and slitter of throats.

Reshef's report of failure did nothing to strike a light.

The darkness deepened.

"What happened?" Narmer asked. "Why didn't the snake succeed?"

"Edmund's magus burst in at the very last second and killed it."

"I ought to kill *him*," Narmer said.

"Yes, my lord," Reshef said. "I could—"

"No, don't. It would draw attention." Narmer leaned back in his
chair. "Do we have any other way to get at her?"

The dark patch that was Reshef shifted from one foot to the other,
not preparing to strike, but out of nervousness. "No, my lord, not here."

Narmer gritted his teeth. "Very well. The hazards of childbirth may yet
save us."

"Yes, my lord."

When Reshef was gone, Narmer called for the captain of his guard.

When the man had presented himself, the potential Pharaoh of the
Two Lands said, "Double tonight's sentries. Don't make a show of it."

"Yes, my lord."

"That will be all."

"Yes, my lord."

The officer left and the tent flap closed.

Narmer drew his battle knife. He clutched it and lay down on his cot.

He tried to sleep, but sleep would not come.

Doubled guard or not, battle knife or not, Narmer was afraid.

But of what?

The question was pointless.

He's already answered it countless times.

He was afraid of death.

No, that wasn't it, not exactly.

He was not afraid of dying, but of being dead. Of not existing. What other fear was there?

With the onset of night, his tent had turned cold, as well as dark. He shivered and pulled his blanket tighter around his shoulders.

That was the problem with the lower river: no matter what time of the year it was, the weather always seemed cold. The locals had to be a rare form of cold-blooded mammal.

It was no good saying that death completed the cosmic cycle: nonexistence, existence, and then a return to nonexistence.

No one but a self-deluded, hopped-up mystic could find solace in that variety of sophistry.

It was the sort of low-level spiritual contortion for which Ulricka had a fondness.

Ulricka.

Would she respond in kind?

Heaven knew she had enough snakes.

TWENTY-SEVEN

The sun climbed above the horizon. The herons hunted in the shallows at the river's edge. The men-at-arms packed up their armor and heavy weapons. They struck and packed their tents. The pavilions came down.

Farewells were exchanged.

It was only polite.

The armies limbered their throwing engines, and they returned their ammunition to its cases.

It made sense.

Vlod's unit positioned the cannons in the center of the field. They loaded them and stopped their barrels, using wooden plugs, driven well home, instead of cement.

The use of wooden plugs rather than cement saved time. Everyone was in a rush.

The witnesses gathered, standing well away.

Using very long fuses, Vlod's crews fired their cannons, one at a time. Bang...Bang...Bang... Until the last was reached. Bang...

Silence.

The cannons were gone.

The rubbish was gathered. The wood was burned, and the metal was set aside for scrap.

The armies called in their skirmishers and posted sentries.

It was only standard procedure.

The stand-down, the joyous peace, left the sourest of glazes on the already bad taste in Dagna's mouth.

She had wanted to fight a war, and now she would have to breed an heir. The prospect disgusted her. It made her feel cheap and without honorable purpose.

She felt as though she had become a party to cowardice.

It was only natural.

Dagna was changing into court dress when Gregory sauntered into her tent, uninvited and unannounced.

Where were her guards?

She was half naked, but she made no attempt to cover herself. If anything, she held herself straighter and arched her back enough to jut her breasts. Why not show them off to their best advantage? Let the bastard have something to remember the next time he rolled around with one of his whores. Let him know she didn't give a damn about him.

Gregory commented on Dagna's finery and the quality of her formal weapon, a dagger with an elephant-ivory handle. Dagna responded with a similar piece of triviality and went out of her way to call peace a distraction from the business of war. "The army's here. We ought to use it."

Gregory said, "You sound disappointed."

"I'd hoped to have my face slashed. Then my father couldn't marry me off."

Gregory drew his battle knife and handed it to her. "There. Newly sharpened."

Balancing it between her fingers, she asked, "What do you expect me to do with this?"

"Cut your face. You can say one of Narmer's people did it."

"I'd rather accuse you."

"No, you wouldn't. Your father would ask too many questions."

"Narmer's people couldn't get this far into our camp."

"Sure they could. Everyone knows what determined little bastards they are."

Dagna returned the weapon. "I have my own knives."

She wormed into her gown, settled it on her shoulders, and smoothed the skirts.

Watching her, he asked, "Will you refuse to marry me?"

"My father requires me to breed with you; therefore, breed with you I shall."

Gregory winced.

Good, she thought. The fool ought to wince.

"I have my charms," he said.

"If I were a whore, you'd be irresistible."

"You have nice tits, by the way. It's too bad you keep them hidden away so much of the time."

She felt her face redden. She'd asked for that, prancing around in front of him.

"Maybe I ought to follow Xenia's example," she said.

"Maybe. You could show her how it's done."

"How what's done?"

"Showing off tits," he said. "You're good at it."

"The nice tits help."

"Indeed they do," he said, and left her tent.

———

Gregory departed for his side of the compound. A few dozen meters away from Dagna's tent, a serving girl was carrying a yoke of water buckets. She came close to blocking the pathway. Gregory jigged around her, and as he did so, he was overcome by a lightness in his step and an insane desire to whistle.

———

Dagna finished dressing. No maid helped her. No friends danced in attendance around her.

She had a good mind to refuse Gregory. She had the right to refuse him. Her father could insist and threaten, but he could not force her to marry Gregory. It was her decision, not his.

She could insist on her admission to the Cathedral's seminary, and in view of recent events, the Mother Metropolitan couldn't very well refuse her.

The goal was within Dagna's grasp. She could run away to the Cathedral and become a priestess.

Yes, but where would be the fun in that?

Outside Edmund's tent, people were running to and fro. Inside, Edmund and Wolfram were doing their best to understand where they had ended up.

"Dagna is the least of your worries," Wolfram said, dismissing that thread.

Edmund splashed a generous amount of Spieden Blue into a glass and handed it to his brother. He poured one for himself and lifted it in a toast. "Better days and kinder fates."

"So and blessed," Wolfram said. He drank and set the glass on the camp table. "How long before they figure out they've fucked themselves?"

"Who?"

"The minor clans."

"How so?"

Rather than spar with his brother, Wolfram answered the question directly. "Sooner or later, your brother chieftains will discover they must come to you for their ships. Apart from Vernon—and maybe the Cathedral—none of them has a competent yard. They'll have to buy from you."

"Anything else?" Edmund asked.

"Like what?"

"They'll tire of the advisory commission and walk away?" Edmund asked. "They do that sort of thing."

Edmund was wrong. The minors might tire of the advisory commission, but they would never tire of the power, of the potential for power it conferred.

Sidestepping, Wolfram asked, "When it comes to walking away, will Vlod walk away from his cannons? Can he?"

"Meaning?"

"Has he got it in him?"

"For his own good, he'd better. Ulricka can't enforce the ban if we thumb our noses at it, but she *must* enforce it if any of us are to survive."

"You'd enforce it on her behalf?"

"I'd have no choice," Edmund said. "It would be his father all over again."

"I understand," Wolfram said, and he did. The clan came first, and without the Mother Metropolitan's blessing, or at the very least her acquiescence, the other clans would descend on Clan Iredale like the jackals they were.

Edmund said, "No amount of success will save him next time. It won't save you, either."

"Me?"

"Yes, you. Not again."

Wolfram shrugged. "Understood. Not again."

—————

Ulricka hosted a celebratory banquet behind the walls of Morven's Gate. It spilled through the dining hall and into a tent, the same one they'd used the day before. From there, it burst out into the open air. The tables, benches, plates, and utensils were the same as before, and the food was the same mix of supplies on-hand, supplies brought in, and "supplies" that had been stupid enough to wander too near on their own four legs.

Early in the evening, Ulricka pleaded fatigue and excused herself.

She insisted that her guests continue without her. It was the gracious thing to do, and with Xenia's tits to entertain them, who was going to miss one waddling old woman?

No one.

In any event, she had work to do.

In her pavilion, Ulricka called for a pot of coffee and sent for Colonel Chiharu, the commander of the Cathedral Guard. She also sent for Shabnan, and she ordered her guards to clear a security perimeter around her pavilion. She voided her bladder and threw herself down into a chair to wait.

The coffee arrived.

The people arrived.

The report that her guards had cleared the perimeter arrived.

Her bladder began to refill.

She felt fat and ugly and middle-aged.

Pregnancy was not a romantic stroll through the Sacred Grove.

She served the coffee herself, and her two guests drank it.

"Why clear the perimeter?" Shabnan asked.

"We need to talk without being overheard," Ulricka said.

Her baby chose that moment to punch and roll.

Weeks and weeks ago these demonstrations of restlessness had given Ulricka a sort of maternal pleasure. But as one internal organ after another had become her baby's personal plaything, the pleasure, the sense of fulfillment, had evaporated.

Ulricka took herself in hand and looked on the bright side. Wasn't that what they told the girls in the Virgins' Pavilion to do when their morning sickness was doubling them over in the latrine? "Look on the bright side, dear. It means that the Goddess has chosen you to bring a new life into the world. What a joy! How blessed you are!"

Ulricka wished that the biddies who dished out that pap had to live with the vomiting, the cramps, the sore backs, the tender breasts, the swollen ankles, and the terror, admitted or denied. When was the last time a breech had ripped one of them apart?

She shuddered at the mental images the words conjured.

In Ulricka's case, her own delivery wouldn't be long now. In a week or two she'd either be alive or dead, a childless mother or a twisted corpse.

Ulricka turned to Chiharu. "The cathedral needs an army. I need an army."

Chiharu's eyes widened in apparent shock. "But, Your Beatitude, you have the Cathedral Guard. They're an accomplished fighting force."

Shabnan smiled and sipped her coffee. Could the good colonel be that stupid?

Ulricka said, "I don't need an 'accomplished fighting force.' I need a blood-and-guts army. I need an army and a navy that can take the field, win battles, and pile heads."

"What about the Cathedral's neutrality?" Chiharu asked.

Shabnan wanted to laugh out loud. Chiharu was skilled, in her way, but she was no strategist. She was the commander of the Cathedral Guard, not the Cathedral's battlemaster. No one was. the Cathedral didn't have a battlemaster, and therein lay the source of the current sucking quagmire. They'd drown in it if Ulricka didn't rise to the occasion and *lead*.

Shabnan asked, "What about a Cathedral staff that's riddled with the likes of Jinhai?"

"Internal security is another matter," Chiharu said. "The main point is that the Cathedral must remain neutral."

When it came to Chiharu, Ulricka didn't like what she was seeing. Chiharu was close to spluttering. It was time to splash on a bucket of cold water.

"Grow up," Ulricka said. "You're the Cathedral's military commander. You're my military commander. Act like it. How do I build an army? How do I *enforce* my neutrality? How do I *enforce* my proscriptions against heresy and disorder?"

Turning directly to Chiharu, Shabnan asked, "In other words, how does Her Beatitude take away their toys and send them to their rooms?"

TWENTY-EIGHT

The morning after the celebratory banquet, the Mother Metropolitan issued her formal permission for Dagna and Gregory to marry.

With the certificates in hand, Gregory and Dagna signed the betrothal contract. The marriage contract would follow in due course.

Ulricka blessed the happy couple and wished them every joy and success.

Shabnan presented them with an illustrated volume on ecstatic fornication.

Gregory leafed through the book, blushed, and expressed his appreciation of the "marvelous gift."

Narmer presented them with his personal Senet board. He embraced Gregory. He embraced Dagna and kissed her on the cheek. It was a polite kiss, a rigid formality.

With that phase of the business concluded, Edmund and Vernon delivered on their promises.

Together with Narmer, Ulricka, and the assorted allied chieftains, Edmund and Vernon signed the treaties needed to implement the negotiated agreements.

As Ulricka signed the last document, a wave of accomplishment washed over her. She'd outmaneuvered Narmer, she'd contained the threat from Edmund and Vernon, and she'd asserted both her authority and her neutrality.

Vlod had already destroyed his cannons in a show of good faith. His drawings and research had to be seized, but beyond that procedural matter, there was only the plodding grind to implement and maintain the treaties.

Work lay ahead, not war.

Ink, not blood.

Ulricka set down the pen...and her water broke.

It soaked the skirt of her gown and splashed across her feet.

The celebration of the new peace had come to a close, but the preparations for another celebration of a new life had just begun.

Ulricka's baby was to be welcomed into the world with as much joy and happiness as possible.

Most were privately relieved or openly joyous.

Others were not.

Rather than push the Cathedral off to one side, Narmer's actions had only served to fortify its position as the region's ultimate arbiter.

Another evening was closing in, but this time Narmer had lit the lamps in his tent before the light had failed, before he had allowed the onrush of time to plunge him into darkness.

A man stood a couple of paces away from him, on the other side of Narmer's worktable. The man was in uniform and he was jittery, as well he might be, given what stood on the opposite side of Narmer's tent.

To mark what was about to happen, Narmer came around his desk and stood where the man could see him without changing position. It was an elevating gesture, a mark of the respect of a superior for a favored subordinate.

"I'm changing your name to Bakari," Narmer said to the immediately former Martinyekev.

The newly minted Bakari was a captain in Narmer's personal guard. He had a reputation for being bright and honest, but not ambitious beyond the call of duty. It was a winning combination in any army, in any court.

"Do you understand?" Narmer asked.

"Yes, my lord," Bakari said.

In addition, and to his credit, his lack of any visible surprise at, or objection to, his new name demonstrated his loyalty and, to be honest, his sagacity.

"*Bakari* means 'noble oath,'" Narmer said. "Do you like it?"

"Yes, my lord."

Narmer didn't give a rat's ass whether Bakari liked his name or loathed it. Of course, he would wear it better if he liked it, but wear it he would. Narmer smile a congratulatory smile. "It goes with your new role as the commander of the Sekhmet Battalion, with the rank of colonel."

"Yes, my lord. Thank you, my lord."

Narmer held out his hand. After only a momentary stutter, Bakari took it, and the two men shook hands.

"Congratulation, Colonel."

"Thank you, my lord."

Narmer broke off the handshake. "Very well. Dismissed."

"Yes, my lord. Thank you, my lord."

Narmer gave their exchange a moment's further thought. "I'm to be addressed as 'Your Majesty' from now on."

Bakari's face went blank, but he covered his mistake with a bow. "Yes, Your Majesty."

"You may go."

"Thank you, Your Majesty."

The man backed out of the tent, bowing repeatedly.

Colonel Bakari might have overdone the bowing, but on reflection, that was a good sign. It meant that as intelligent as he was, he could find himself at a loss. Not a bad thing in a subordinate.

Bakari had entered Narmer's tent a promising young captain and had exited it the promising young commander of the Sekhmet Battalion, with the rank of colonel.

Lieutenant colonels, not colonels, commanded battalions; but Narmer had made an exception in this case. Generosity did no harm and might do a lot of good.

Narmer sat down behind his worktable.

For the next several minutes, he looked at the two heads on the points of the two spears on the opposite side of his tent.

Of the two, Harakhty's was the worse for wear. It was multihued: an ominous shade of purple, a repellent brown, and a putrescent color that might pass for yellow. A score of flies buzzed around it. They landed and crawled, fed and laid their eggs.

The other head, Reshef's, had attracted a no less numerous and no less industrious cloud of the insects, but so far Reshef's coloration had held up, and he hadn't yet begun to stink.

Harakhty's head reeked.

Sad but true, the bloom had gone off Harakhty's rose.

The bloom had also gone off Reshef's, in that he no longer amused. The time had come to forgive and forget.

Narmer called in the sergeant of his guard.

"Yes, my lord?"

Narmer pointed at the two heads. "Throw those into the nearest cesspit."

Ulricka's labor was no less miserable than it had been the last time she'd given birth, but in due course, it culminated in the emergence of a baby boy into the waking world.

The moment the cord was cut and tied, he was removed for genetic examination.

Ulricka closed her eyes and ignored her attendants. Let them fuss. Let them cluck, and coo, and bustle. It made them feel needed. They weren't, but it was important that they felt as though they were.

Ulricka tried not to think about what the geneticist was doing to the baby: the evaluation of skin tone and coloration; the search for untoward blemishes; the counts of fingers, toes, eyes, ears, and limbs; the palpating; and the tests of reflexes, sensory responses, and motor strength.

Were the eyes clear or clouded, dull or bright, jaundiced or healthy? So much depended on the eyes!

The fussbudgets were preferable.

Several minutes later, Quintana, the Cathedral's geneticist, came back into the room. Her face was neither joyful nor grave. Hers was a neutral smile, very clinical, very much a mask.

Quintana was middle-aged. She had dried up years ago, and her breasts had sagged. Her hair hung in a gray-and-black braid to her waist. She exuded an odor of medicine and another of the overly spiced sausages she'd recently eaten.

Beyond garlic, the odors were too overpowering, too much of an assault, to identify. They were a blur, an avalanche—as sickening as they were repulsive.

Normally, geneticists were drawn from the magi, who were exclusively male; however, Quintana had been trained by and admitted to the Geneticists Guild without first being trained as a magus and admitted to the College of Magi. This followed an age-old pattern and was one of the many ways in which the Cathedral and the College of Magi maintain the wary and jealous peace that pertained between them.

Ulricka propped herself up on one elbow. "Have I given birth to a Child of the Cathedral or to a weakling?" It was the required, ritual question. "A boy, wasn't it?"

They could tell her no more about him, and she could ask no more. To do either meant condemnation and death. No one was exempt from this rule. The Children of the Cathedral must remain anonymous, their parents unrecorded and unremembered.

Outside Ulricka's pavilion, the crowd was hushed.

Was it a good sign or a bad one?

Warrick, the Iredales' geneticist and the most senior member of the guild present, slipped in behind Quintana. He smiled at Ulricka.

But wouldn't he smile regardless of the outcome? Wasn't it the way of geneticists to reassure, to pretend that the situation was as it should be, no matter the horror that the woman may have delivered?

Quintana said, "You have given the Cathedral a baby boy, Your Beatitude."

Ulricka felt the tension go out of her. Every muscle had been tight, strained to the point of spasm, and then, with the announcement of a good outcome, they had given up their hold. She was able to breathe again without that cursed shallow panting. She had a thousand questions, but she dare not ask any of them.

A boy. Healthy. Not a weakling. It would have to do. As it always did.

Quintana asked, "May we announce the birth?"

"Please," Ulricka said.

"Your court, the entire province will rejoice for you," Warrick said.

The man's voice was too smooth, too much like the skin of a rattlesnake.

"Thank you," Ulricka said.

The midwife changed the worst of the bed linen, and Ulricka was at last able to lean back onto her pillows and rest.

One by one, the people left the room.

Shabnan stayed. She pulled a chair close and sat down. "Do you want anything?"

"Thank you, no."

Now, Ulricka thought, now the agony begins.

She stopped herself. The separation from her baby—no, he was the Cathedral's baby! The separation from the baby was inevitable and necessary.

Because she was the avatar of the Goddess, Ulricka was the mother of all, and because she was the mother or all, she could be the mother of no particular child.

But with this child, for no reason that she could fathom, her selfish yearnings had turned strident. She *wanted* him. She wanted *her* baby.

"You're brooding," Shabnan said. She grimaced in self-deprecation. "Sorry about the pun."

Ulricka wanted to smile, wanted to rise above her roiling emotions, but she couldn't.

"I want to nurse my baby," she said. Her throat tightened and her eyes burned.

"Like as not, you will," Shabnan said.

Shabnan's statement contained a measure of truth, but it also contained a dose of cruelty. Over the next few weeks, Ulricka would serve as a wet nurse to a score of the Cathedral's infants, but never to the same one twice. Nor would the nursery attendants, on pain of summary execution, ever tell her which baby in that procession of babies was hers and which was not.

Because they had taken hers away from her the moment she had given birth to him, recognition, certain recognition, would be impossible.

Still, recognition—by a mother of her child—must have happened in the past, and from time to time, she had had her own hunches about this one or that one, but the iron rule of anonymity had remained inviolate. Recognition was not fact, and rare was the mother, mother metropolitan or not, who was stupid enough to speculate openly.

Her voice breaking, Ulricka said, "When I nurse him, I want to know he's mine."

Shabnan sighed. "You can't."

"Why not?"

"Because *you* say so."

Xenia snuggled closer to Vernon. She twisted her face against his chest. Women could be fun, yes, and comfortable, and on the whole she preferred them as lovers, without a doubt in the world, but men scratched the primal itch in a way that women could not. Maybe it was all that muscle and hair, the touch of callused hands, the dominance without domination, the incipient danger, the risk of pregnancy.

The desire for pregnancy.

Now there was an unsettling thought.

Both frightening and arousing.

Ulricka's machinations made absurd pillow talk, but Vernon had asked about what the Mother Metropolitan, or one of her bootlickers, might do to her.

Was he concerned for her or no better than curious?

"I'm safe for a while," Xenia said. "Ulricka never does anything she might need to undo."

Xenia playfully bit one of Vernon's nipples. She heard the quick intake of his breath when she sucked on it. She let go of it and said, "I don't need to worry about assassination. She won't order it, and my brother's too much of a coward to go down that road."

She lay her head back down. They'd return to the fun and games later. For the moment, she wanted to bask in the animal warmth of his body, to luxuriate in the rumble of his voice as he spoke. No woman's voice did that.

"She may fool you," Vernon said.

"You can tell her for me that I've decided not to be Mother Metropolitan."

"Have you?"

"I have."

"What will you do with yourself instead?"

"I shall do all that I can to support my brother in the desperate struggle ahead."

Vernon laughed. "Who says there's going to be one?"

"Peace, O warrior among men, is a one-word oxymoron."

TWENTY-NINE

Vlod was glad to be away from Morven's Gate.

He, Edmund, and Wolfram rode at the head of a small cavalry detachment. They were on their way back to the manor, back to Castle Olney, by the most direct route, the overland road, rather than by the tracks that followed along the riverbank.

Wolfram had ordered the army to embark and return home by river. A garrison of the usual strength was to remain at Morven's Gate.

Of Vlod, Edmund asked, "About the cannons, where are the plans and other documents?"

"In my rooms," Vlod said. "I'll hand them over to whomever Ulricka sends."

Wolfram asked, "Fine, but won't they enable her to build cannons of her own?"

It was a reasonable question, one Vlod had wanted to ask but couldn't, not without descending into a maelstrom of accusation and counter-accusation. "They might."

"Will they or won't they?" Wolfram demanded. "This is no time for *mights*."

"In theory, they would," Vlod said. "But she won't."

"Why not?"

"The threat of retaliation."

"From whom?" Wolfram asked. "She'd have Narmer's support."

"You misunderstand Narmer," Edmund said. "He'd be the first to stick her head on a pike. He wants the Cathedral."

"What's he going to do with it?"

"At a guess, rededicate it to the Egyptian pantheon," Edmund said. "The so-called Two Lands are the least of his ambitions. He wants the Province as a province."

"He wants his bones to lie in a pyramid," Vlod said. "He wants to ride in Ra's boat."

Wolfram shrugged his acceptance of the point they were making. "In that case, Ulricka is his greatest obstacle."

"That she is," Edmund said, "which is why we must be her greatest allies."

They rode on in silence for a time.

"What about your cannons, Vlod?" Edmund asked. "Sorry to see them go?"

To Vlod's own surprise, he said, "They were a distraction."

"From what?" Wolfram asked.

"Pumping water."

Thirty

A slow, leisurely dinner, graced by as much peace and quiet as Olney Castle had to offer.

Edmund and his brother ate on the terrace that opened off the castle's private dining room. Because the terrace faced to the north, toward the river, Edmund seldom used it except in high summer. For those few weeks, it was cool enough to be comfortable and warm enough to be pleasant.

Weeks?

High summer on Clan Iredale land was closer to days than it was to weeks.

Edmund drained his wine glass and refilled it. Thus far, they'd talked about sailboats—sloops versus cutters, canoe sterns versus transom sterns—but he wanted to change the subject, and so he did. "Do you believe in necromancy?"

"No," Wolfram said. "Dead is dead." He added, "At any rate, inaccessible to the living. The dead live on in their world, and we live in ours."

"What if necromancy *were* a possibility?" Edmund asked. "Maybe the dead could answer a few questions for us, or maybe they need to hear how much we love them."

"Are you talking about Morven?"

"We were up at his gate. I started to wonder."

"You'd be wading into quicksand."

"Possibly."

"He can't tell you who killed him," Wolfram said. "Correction: He *may* not be able to."

"Who better?" Edmund asked.

"The person who did. If Hamlet's father was asleep when Claudius poured the poison into his ear, how did Hamlet's father know it was Claudius? He couldn't have seen him."

"The play explains that, doesn't it?"

"Don't pick nits."

"Morven *may* have seen him," Edmund said. "It may have been face-to-face."

"He may have seen the man who wielded the sword."

"I see your point. Who wielded the man?"

"That's the important question, isn't it?"

"True, enough, but I want to try," Edmund said.

Wolfram drained his glass and refilled it. "Try away, but I suspect that the dead tell as many lies to the living as the living tell to the Gods...or to one another."

"Morven wouldn't lie to me," Edmund said.

"He might if it were for your own good."

"Now you're telling me what you would do. Morven wouldn't lie to me."

Wolfram had his doubts, but he said, "He may not have the whole truth. He may be mistaken. What makes the dead any less fallible than the living?"

"They see things we don't. Life doesn't obscure things from them."

To that piece of romanticism, Wolfram had no answer. He said, "Vlod's a magus. He's no necromancer, but he ought to be familiar with the outlines."

"The magi are fonts of insight," Edmund said sourly.

"Why not talk it over with him?"

"Because he's busy."

<hr>

Mother Charlotte lived in the rectory attached to the Manor Henge of Desdemona the Shipbreaker, the manor henge of Clan Iredale. Her apartment was on the upper floor, and her sitting room small. It was neither pokey nor drab nor crowded, but neither was it overloaded with a desk, several bookcases, a table, and two sideboards. Instead, it was a comfortable space—a fireplace, a braided rug on the plank floor, a single bookcase, a potted plant, a vase of flowers in front of the window, upholstered chairs, a small writing desk, and the pervasive aromas of fresh-brewed tea and recent baking.

One of the housemaids had shown Vlod into the room and told him to make himself comfortable. Mother Charlotte would be with him soon.

Vlod picked a chair and sat in it. It looked as though it might not be Mother Charlotte's favorite, as though it would be one of the chairs intended for guests to use.

The trace of a draft puffed down the chimney and fluttered, ever so slightly, the ash in the fireplace. The smell of ash, or of last night's fire, tiptoed into the room.

The door swung open and Mother Charlotte entered.

Vlod rose, she smiled, and they exchanged ritual kisses on the cheeks.

She was in her late forties, and common knowledge had it that twenty-five years ago she'd refused election to the metropolitanate, claiming that she wanted to stay on the coast, close to saltwater. If they'd agree to relocate the Cathedral to Fort George, then she'd agree to be the Mother Metropolitan, but if not, then not. They hadn't, and she hadn't, and here she was.

"What brings you to me?" she asked.

"She's approved my petition," Vlod said, handing over Ulricka's letter.

"What wonderful news," Mother Charlotte said happily. She appeared to be genuinely pleased.

She unfolded the letter and read.

When she had finished, she refolded the letter and put it into a pocket within the folds of her robe.

"Success at last," she said. "I'm glad for him, and I'm glad for you."

"Thank you."

"By now you've heard it hundreds of times, but your father was an outstanding intellect. What they did to him was shameful."

"He'd be pleased to hear you say so."

"He did," she said. "I visited him the night before. We had a wonderful talk, given the circumstances."

She led Vlod out of her residence, across the manor henge, and down into the dirge grotto.

She interrupted the dirge singers and directed Vlod to the lectern.

"Please," she said, and motioned for him to chant. "I believe he would want you to be the first."

Vlod squared himself to the book and chanted his father's name: *Shivananda the Magus*.

He drew out the syllables. He lifted and dropped them through the notes, as his instructors had taught him at the Academy, but his voice came out as an arid croak.

The dirge singers smiled graciously, but their consternation was plain in the set of the lines around their mouths. The name of a notorious heretic read into the *Dirge*? It was unheard of! It was outrageous! What was Mother Charlotte doing?

A minute or two later, Vlod and Mother Charlotte were walking toward the front gate of the manor henge.

Mother Charlotte said, "Don't worry about the paperwork. You've chanted your father's name into the *Dirge*, and I've documented it. You have assured his place among the Gods and the Generations. We'll forward the recording on the first packet."

"Thank you," Vlod said, and left the henge.

His boots crunched on the graveled road.

Despite what he had expected to feel, he didn't feel one damn bit better.

His father was still dead, still the victim of a judicial murder.

Vernon sent for his physician.

They met in Vernon's private apartments, in Vernon's dayroom, alone and at night.

The room was stuffy, confining, and Vernon wished he could be somewhere else, anywhere else.

The man asked questions, and Vernon answered them. The man poked and prodded, and Vernon cooperated. The man asked for samples of Vernon's blood, urine, semen, and stool. Vernon provided them, and the man examined them.

He asked more questions, tested reflexes, looked deep into Vernon's eyes, and performed a digital rectal exam.

Vernon's physician washed his hands and gave Vernon his findings: Vernon was dying of cancer.

"How long do I have?" Vernon asked.

"I can't say for sure. Months. A year. Two. I had one patient I was certain had gone into remission. He hadn't. I had another I thought would die within a couple of months. He lasted for five years. Cancer, my lord, is not cancer is not cancer is not cancer. It's best thought of as a family of diseases. Some are slow, and some are fast."

"When will you be able to give me a better figure?"

"In a few weeks, if ever."

Vernon thanked the man and went out onto the balcony of his dayroom. It was far into a moonless night.

The city walls ran down to the river, along the beach, and then cut back inland. They circled around, like the arms of a protective mother. Watch fires burned on the watchtowers. They made the wall look like a necklace of dancing topaz-colored jewels.

He thought about his situation and decided he could tell no one until after the wedding. To do so would be to invite the vultures, and they, being the darlings that they were, would rend the carcass before it was dead.

Vernon wasn't dead yet, not for some months. A year or two. Or five months.

Regardless of how long it turned out to be, would it be long enough?

When it came to his sons, he had much to take in hand. Too much. He'd put it off, and now he'd run out of time. He would have to intervene. He would have to forge his boys into men.

Quickly.

He had five months.

Two years.

Maybe.

However it played out, his time was short.

He sent for his magus.

The man arrived, and they talked in Vernon's dayroom.

Vernon ordered him to perform an augury. That very night. He was to use a human victim and he was to employ the services of a vision dancer.

"My lord?" the man asked. His voice rasped with the leftovers of interrupted sleep. "A *human* victim, my lord?"

"I have a human problem," Vernon said, "and I require a human answer."

"Yes, my lord," his magus said. "I'll send word when I've completed the necessary preparations."

"Tell no one of this."

"Yes, my lord. No one, my lord. Very good, my lord."

The cringing weasel bowed his way out.

Vernon returned to his balcony, but in a matter of moments, he returned to his dayroom.

A single-wicked lamp burned on his desk.

In the morning, he'd exchange it for one with three wicks, a three-wicked lamp to blind the Wandering Night Spirits.

Vernon scoffed at the practice, the product of rank superstition.

It was the prospect of death that brought out such behaviors. He'd seen it among sailors and men-at-arms before a battle, before a voyage, before a storm. He'd never expected to see it in himself.

What further pointless rituals and ridiculous obsessions would he indulge in before he died?

He bade his newly arrived superstitious nature a hearty welcome.

It accepted his greeting. It tried out the furniture and it admired the decor. It put its feet up and it settled in.

Vernon returned to his balcony and watched the embracing string of fiery topaz-colored jewels.

As he watched them, his thoughts wandered, but then settled on a single dilemma. He couldn't make up his mind whether he was happy about his newly arrived tenant or not.

THIRTY-ONE

August evicted July. The two months had been named for two ancient emperors, one assassinated, the other his avenger and successor.

August swept the floors, cleaned the draperies, and took up residence.

By coastal norms, the weather was warm and dry, the winds moderate. True, the days were shortening toward the autumnal equinox, which, if the Cathedral and manor henges performed the rites with care, would arrive in September.

Everyone knew perfectly well that the Wheel of the Year would turn whether the rites were performed or not. But it would not turn in quite the same way. A vital but ineffable element would be absent without those ritual blessings. The days would pass, one after the other, but they would do no more than plod by. They would come and go without any sense of quickening purpose, without sparkle, without the Goddess's blessing.

It was a gentle season, quiet in its own way, but this year, no one could afford to relax.

Thanks to the war that hadn't happened, the clan was working double shifts to split and stack firewood; to dry, smoke, and salt fish and meat; to repair and repaint buildings, walls, and ships; to throw and fire pottery; to tuck-point masonry; to repair roofs and replace missing shingles; and to complete the thousands upon thousands of other tasks essential to prepare for the approaching, inevitable winter.

Vlod unlocked his workshop. He went inside and closed the door, leaving it on the latch. Sunlight stabbed in around the boards covering the windows. Vlod lit a whale-oil lamp and hung it on a peg.

The room was much as he had left it months ago. Dust had accumulated, right enough, but the twisted pipes and the bent plates, the wreckage of the boiler and water tank, lay in the heap where Vlod had thrown them.

The door scraped open.

Vlod gripped the handle of his sword and turned to face the intruder.

Ziellottes entered. He closed the door. This time it made no sound.

The man's skill never failed to amaze Vlod. No doubt the old spy could smash a water jug against a stone wall without making the slightest sound.

"I've been talking with Edmund," Ziellottes said, and advanced into the workshop.

Vlod opened his hand and eased it away from his sword.

Ziellottes used the toe of his boot to prod the pile of scrap. "Your water pump?"

"Someday," Vlod said.

Ziellottes gave the pile a vigorous nudge. It clanked. "Not with this kind of junk."

"It was what I had available."

"You scrounged. You hoped to draw as little attention as possible."

"That, too."

"Caution isn't like you," Ziellottes said.

"Maybe I'm not the flash grenade you think I am."

"What an interesting term, *flash grenade*."

"I've been reading."

"Is there no end to your crimes?"

"I hope not," Vlod said.

"What have you been reading?"

"Old books," Vlod said.

"Dreaming dreams?"

"Doing my best to avoid an ancient nightmare."

Ziellottes rolled his eyes. "From the man who resurrected the cannon. Forgive me if I cherish my skepticism."

A jibe or a warning? Vlod asked, "What are you doing here?"

"Water pumps will free Edmund's servants from countless hours of drudgery, but they won't thank you for it. In fact, they may well murder you for it. Thank you very much, runt; now die, you loathsome miscreant."

"I don't want their thanks."

"How marvelously wise of you. There are two things people never want. They don't want anyone to tell them awkward truths, and they don't want anyone to free them from bondage. They prefer lies and slavery, as long as the lies soothe and the chains don't chafe." Ziellottes picked up a short, flat piece of iron. He turned it over, then righted it. "Your father tried to tell them the truth, and they murdered him for it." He dropped the iron back onto the pile. It banged, bounced, and rattled. "I fear for your longevity."

"Come to the point."

"That was the point. Did you miss it?"

No, Vlod hadn't missed it, but he said, "What else?"

Ziellottes' expression turned serious. "I've told Edmund, but I don't trust him to tell you."

A gambit or the truth? Rather than play the loyal subordinate and refuse to listen, Vlod asked, "Tell me what?"

"Vernon has cancer. He's dying."

THIRTY-TWO

A week later, Hadwyn, the Cathedral's engineer and, at the moment, the Mother Metropolitan's personal envoy, arrived by trireme from Maryhill.

Vlod watched him come ashore. He was a tall, robust man, precisely dressed. He had brown hair and a thick beard, both curled. He came down the gangplank like an excited child.

Stepping onto the dock, he turned this way and that, and then, as though he had just discovered where he was, he strode toward Edmund.

A late summer breeze flitted across the harbor in teasing gusts. It was a warm breeze, but it carried a decided hint of the approaching fall. The gusts playfully billowed and rolled the overly large provincial ensign that was flying from the stern of the trireme.

"He's young," Wolfram said.

"He's arrogant," Edmund said.

"She never sends any other sort," Wolfram said.

"She sent the Crone," Vlod said.

"True. She's arrogant, but not young."

Hadwyn came to a parade-ground halt a couple of meters before Edmund and bowed precisely.

The moment the introductions were over, Hadwyn demanded that

Edmund turn over "any and all designs, diagrams, and research notes in your possession or in your clan's possession regarding or touching upon the conception, construction, operation, or use of gunpowder-based, gunpowder-fired, or gunpowder-inspired weapons."

Edmund's expression of polite acceptance vanished, and Vlod wondered if Ulricka's puppy had any idea what the abrupt hardness around Edmund's eyes meant.

Hadwyn was in danger of convincing Edmund to send him home in a sack.

To be sure, Edmund would include Vlod's notes and designs. A deal was a deal, but the Iredale chieftain had never promised to allow Ulricka, or any of her lackeys, to treat him like a disobedient child.

"If you please, my lord," the puppy added.

Edmund said, "It pleases me to hand them over, but the truth is, we didn't expect you and haven't assembled them."

The puppy's eyebrows shot up.

"My lord, if I may?" Vlod said.

"Granted," Edmund said.

To Hadwyn, Vlod said, "It's my fault, and I do most humbly apologize." He wanted to sound muddled and flustered, eccentric, but he didn't dare lay it on too thick. Ulricka would have seen through such playacting instantly, but this perfumed fop, this hobbyist in the affairs of state, never would. "You see, the papers are scattered right across the manor. They're safe enough in their current locations, but we did disburse them: to the powder mill, a blacksmith shop, the wainwrights, and so forth and so on. I—"

"Why haven't you assembled them into one place?" Hadwyn asked. "You were fully aware that I'd be arriving to assume custody of them."

"Indeed, we did, very, very much so. The Autumnal Equinox will soon be upon us, and Her Beatitude will wish to have this sorry business concluded by then."

"Indeed she will."

"Yes, indeed, but I was afraid they might offer too tempting a target were I to assemble them together into one place."

"A target for whom?"

"Why, for spies!" Vlod shook his head sadly. "Despite our peaceful times, spies and saboteurs are ubiquitous."

"When will the papers be ready?"

"Tonight. Tomorrow morning at the latest."

Edmund cocked an eyebrow. "Tomorrow morning? That will never do. Make it tonight, if you know what's good for you."

"Yes, my lord," Vlod said. "It shall be done, my lord."

To Hadwyn, Edmund said, "I'll hold a banquet tonight. I'm sure that before it's over, Vlod will have delivered the specified materials to you."

"That will be acceptable, my lord," Hadwyn said.

Edmund assigned a detail to escort the Cathedral's engineer to his suite in the castle.

Wolfram went with them.

Edmund and Vlod were alone on the dock.

"You've had those papers in your rooms for days," Edmund said, his voice low.

"If I'd told him I'd assembled the materials ahead of time, he'd have asked why."

"It's a good question. Why did you?"

"To cull out the materials that shouldn't fall into Narmer's hands." Vlod added, "It's an old ploy. If I'd had them on hand, he would have made it appear that I shouldn't have assembled them. If I'd not had them on hand, he would have made it appear that I should have gathered them up days ago and bound them together with a pretty ribbon."

"I wish I trusted you as much as I used to."

"Shall I resign?"

Edmund shook his head. "When it's time, if it comes to that, I'll tell you."

———

Ulricka strolled through Thora's greenhouse, her Crystal Palace. In the event, the structure hadn't turned out to be as large as Thora had planned, but it was big enough. It held eighteen orange trees, arranged in three rows. They were larger than saplings but a full decade away from bearing fruit.

The air was moist. It was not rain-forest humid or clammy, but neither was it desiccated or overheated, the sort of air that surrounded the building.

The water vapor rose from the irrigated soil, and it was held aloft by the warmth in the air. The rooftop vents were open, ensuring the circulation of the air, ensuring the proper balances between heat and cold, moisture and aridity.

Over the years, swallows had nested in the rafters, and Ulricka delighted in watching them, especially in the evenings when they went after whatever insects they could find.

The place smelled of damp earth, fertilizer, orange trees, and birds. The colors were dark green and a variety of rich browns, the gray of the gravel underfoot, and the white of the painted frames that held the panes of glass. The sound of her sandals on the gravel was the only sound, apart from the whisper of the swallows' wings.

Outside, the world was rushing toward whatever destiny awaited it, but in here, in Thora's greenhouse, that frantic chaos had been supplanted by the steady faith of one woman and sixteen trees.

The door to Vlod's rooms swung open and Wolfram entered. The odor of tobacco smoke clung to him like an invisible fog.

Vlod made no effort to hide the document he was copying. "How's the banquet?" he asked.

"Winding down," Wolfram said, and closed the door. He threw the bolt and dropped into a chair. "Your door was unlocked. I could have been anybody."

"Not you," Vlod said.

"You magi are such incredible simpletons," Wolfram said.

"The sound of your tread is yours and yours alone."

Wolfram made a disbelieving face. "Are you ready to make your entrance?"

"Nearly," Vlod said.

"Hurry."

"I'm working as fast as I can."

"Work faster. Hadwyn's making noises about coming to find you."

"That would never do."

A moment later, Vlod finished copying the last line on the last page.

"There. I'm finished!"

He'd been at work at his redaction for days, and his hands ached. He set his pen down and massaged his fingers and wrists.

"Nothing like the prospect of a warm fire to comfort the inner man," Wolfram said. "She'll burn us, if she ever finds out."

"Pessimist."

"Realist."

Vlod sighed. "Edmund, too, I'm afraid."

Wolfram nodded his acceptance of that dismal point. "We're taking a huge risk."

"We have *no* choice."

"He wouldn't take it," Wolfram said.

"He's a believer," Vlod said.

"More's the pity," Wolfram said. "Tell me, what do you believe in?"

The answer came automatically. "Necessity."

"There are worse gods."

Vlod imagined that he ought to respond, but he'd tired of the topic. And he had a job to finish.

He considered the two stacks of paper on his desk. The one on the left contained perhaps a hundred irregular sheets. Many were torn, most were smudged and sloppy, scribbled, abbreviated to a fault, stick figures rather than sketches, never mind drawings. They were working papers, not plans or documentation.

In contrast, the stack on the right *was* documentation. It contained better than two hundred crisp, new sheets. They were Vlod's most recent handiwork.

He had expanded the original notes.

In the process of copying, he had produced texts, references. He had filled in the half-thoughts, and he had completed the sketches. He had added captions and annotations. He had expanded the explanations and added detail to the speculations.

Wolfram held out a silver hipflask. The top had been screwed off. "Here, calm your nerves."

The brandy was strong, and its flaring warmth pulled Vlod's attention away from the abomination he was committing.

"Have you heard about Vernon?" Wolfram asked.

Vlod decided to play dumb. "What about him?"

"Have another drink," Wolfram said. "The captain of Hadwyn's ship is an old gossip. He says Vernon has cancer."

"What do Vernon's people say?"

"Not a word."

"What about your people?" Vlod asked. His second sip went down as politely as the first. "What do they say?"

"Nothing. It isn't as if they haven't had their ears open."

"It's true, then."

"Likely true," Wolfram said.

Vlod returned the flask. "Thanks."

"My pleasure," Wolfram said. "You're the one taking the immediate risks."

"It's my duty to take them, just as it's yours to protect Edmund."

"The Iredales. I protect the Iredales."

"Edmund is the Iredales."

"No, there's a difference. Always remember that Edmund is *not* the clan he leads."

"That's dangerous ground."

"Dangerous and then some, but it's the bedrock truth. I'm the clan's battlemaster, not the clan's army. I may command, but they have to do the obeying."

Vlod was too tired, too rattled to plunge into that thicket. He'd already slipped and slid around its edges, which had added enough discomfort to a night already filled with bone-chilling terror.

Vlod stuffed the originals into a dispatch bag. He fastened the latch and handed it to Wolfram. "Make my excuses, will you? I've taken ill."

"Summer flu or bad fish?" Wolfram asked.

"Flu. I don't want Hadwyn to drop in."

"Remember to wash the ink off your hands," Wolfram said.

Vlod shrugged. "My hands are always ink-stained." Like a storm-driven wave breaking over a stricken ship, a limitless fatigue crashed down on him. "You're right, though. Too much fresh ink would look bad."

"You're not as guileless as you pretend," Wolfram said, and opened the door.

Vlod couldn't let the battlemaster go, not yet. "I need to tell you—"

Wolfram stopped and turned back into the room. "Tell me what?"

"That I understand why you and Edmund had to abandon my father's cause."

"You've grown up, then," Wolfram said, and left, closing the door behind him.

Vlod threw the bolt, not for safety but for privacy.

Vlod returned to his desk, and eased into his chair. He felt dazed. If he tried to stand, he'd stagger and collapse. His muscles vibrated like loose halyards in a high wind.

Well, let them.

His mind drifted.

It ranged here and there, essentially at will, but the pile of copies soon captured his attention. It took little effort to picture Ulricka using them to kindle the fire that would end his life. After all, she had to have realized that he would preserve his work against a time of direr need. And such a time *was* coming, marching down upon them at Narmer's bidding.

The want-to-be Pharaoh's ego was part of it, but it was not the important part, not the part that would drive him and his armies forward.

Sadly, the logic of Narmer's situation, the necessity of his very geography demanded that he control the river, that he gain and hold unrestricted access to deep water, to the Pacific trade routes. He could not allow his clan to choke to death. He could not allow it to strangle, bottled up behind the dams, behind the Cathedral, and behind the Columbia River bar.

He must own the gauntlet, not run it.

When his attack came, as come it must, Ulricka would not be able to stop Narmer. But neither could she allow him to succeed, nor could she allow Edmund to stop him with the use of cannons.

That ancient heresy, cannons, would end everything she stood for, everything in which she believed. Were she to allow it, her life would have meant nothing, the cathedral would have meant nothing.

Vlod locked his copies away behind a wall panel. He'd installed it himself, in secret, but it would only delay a search, not foil it.

He would have to find a better hiding place for his copies. Away from his rooms, away from the possibility of an accidental discovery, away from a determined search, away from Olney Castle.

Not tonight.

Tonight he had other business.

He washed his face and scrubbed as much of the ink from his hands as possible.

He wanted to believe that between the two of them—he and Wolfram —they had changed the rules of heresy, but they'd done no such thing. The rules of heresy weren't theirs to change.

Vlod put on his best robe. It would be politic for him to experience an unexpected recovery. It must have been what he'd eaten for lunch and not the flu. He was feeling much better. What luck!

A wave of nausea roiled his stomach.

He returned to the washstand.

He picked up his hairbrush and looked at himself in the mirror.

The face he saw was his face, but it was also a stranger's face.

He had betrayed Edmund.

He had betrayed Ulricka.

He had betrayed his own beliefs in what it was to be a magus and a warrior.

Maybe the owner of the face in the mirror deserved to go up in smoke.

There was no *maybe* about it. The little shit looking back at him deserved to die.

Would Wolfram betray him?

If needs be.

Wolfram would have no trouble, not a trace, in choosing between the life of a magus and the welfare of the clan. The clan would win, and rightly so.

It was the price they'd agreed to.

It was the price of survival.

The candle on Vlod's desk guttered out.

In the dark, he studied what he could see of his reflection.

He brushed his hair into an imitation of order, neither neat nor disheveled. It was the hair of a magus who had recovered from a mild case of food poisoning. It had to have been the fish. Incredible. Unheard of. A once-in-a-lifetime experience.

He straightened his robes. He must look the part of a proper magus, loyal to the College of Magi and to his guild, the Guild of Augurs, dedicated to the service of his chieftain. He must present the very epitome of prescience, intellect, and honor.

It was a worthy goal, but nowhere in his reflection could he find that man.

He saw another man instead, an altogether different man. Older. Unwilling to turn back, unwilling to complain, unwilling to lie, unwilling to save himself.

"I have become my father," Vlod said, and went downstairs to join the banquet.

THIRTY-THREE

Ulricka lifted the crying baby boy from Shabnan's arms.

His cries filled Ulricka's private bedchamber, the one room in her apartments in the Saraswati Palace where she could be alone, where she could close herself off from her attendants. The room was too warm and too airless, the windows closed, the door locked.

The baby thrashed and kicked, and Ulricka was afraid she might drop him if he didn't settle down. What was wrong with him?

At least he smelled like a baby, rather than like an unemptied chamber pot.

His clothes and blanket were clean.

They must have given him a bath before they sent him over.

She counted his fingers and toes, and she inspected his arms and legs. She checked the set and cast of his eyes. They were brown, the whites still blue.

"He's healthy," Shabnan said.

Ulricka heard a faint trace of amusement in the Crone's voice.

The baby's howling rose to a shriek.

Ulricka tucked her fingers between his diaper and his tummy. She searched from side to side. No pins. Well, then...

She rocked him and shushed him.

Pillar to post in the nursery. Lucky to have anyone to hold him, to cuddle him, to take care of him. The Cathedral treated its animals with greater care.

"Mine?" she asked. "You're sure he's mine?"

"He's yours," Shabnan said, but offered no details. "I wouldn't have brought you someone else's baby."

"You're sure he's mine?"

"You're repeating yourself. Yes. I'm sure."

It was assurance enough.

"He's so ugly," Ulricka said.

"He's hungry. They haven't fed him in hours."

"Why not?"

"They wanted him to be hungry for you."

"Toadies," Ulricka said. She opened her dress, exposing a breast. "They don't know, do they?"

"Who he is? No. His hunger has nothing to do with you personally. It's a new procedure. The wet nurses have complained about frequent feedings. As far as the toadies are concerned, he's with a wet nurse."

"They can never find out."

"They won't. Layers upon layers. Wheels within wheels. You're safe."

Ulricka brought the baby around and tickled his face with her nipple. He twisted toward her, closed his mouth on her nipple, and began to suck. He closed his eyes.

Within moments, an unfamiliar but remembered joy came over her.

She babbled to him, her voice pitched high. "Didn't those nasty old ladies feed you? Didn't they give you anything to eat at all?"

The baby shifted and wormed in closer.

She saw a red splotch on his head, right behind his left ear. A birthmark? No, it was too angry for a birthmark, raw and inflamed.

"What have they done to you?" she asked.

Careful not to disturb him, she shifted him so she could get a better look.

Almost.

She waited, not daring to move farther.

The rhythm of his sucking and breathing didn't change.

Ulricka bent her head forward. There it was. The mark. Her stomach turned.

A sudden rush of anger threatened to overpower her. The splotch was a burn, blistered and hideous.

How could such a thing have taken place?

Who would have done such a squalid thing to a baby?

She then saw that the burn was not just any mark. It was a double-bitted axe, the labrys of the Goddess.

Pointing, she demanded, "What happened here?"

"I branded him," Shabnan said.

Ulricka felt the blood drain from her face. Her body tensed, and the baby squirmed. Patting his back, she resettled him.

Shabnan said, "I used the handle of one of the small candle snuffers we use in the cathedral. They have the labrys in bas-relief on them. I heated it in a flame, and I pressed it onto the skin behind his ear."

Ulricka tried to speak, tried to protest, but the words stalled in her throat.

Shabnan said, "I made it look like an accident, and the attendants in the nursery were so stupid that they believed it."

"Get out of my sight!"

Shabnan touched the baby's head with the backs of her fingers. "Don't worry. He'll grow up believing the story of the accident: how the snuffer slipped and it burned him. Marked for life, poor dear. Such a shame. I ought to be horsewhipped."

"You ought to be charged!"

"Perhaps, but you won't do it."

"Why not?"

"Because from now on you'll be able to pick him out."

Ulricka felt her eyes go wide in shock. "What kind of a monster are you?"

"The kind who's made it possible for you to love one of your own children...and for him, in time, to mourn your death, and to cherish your memory, and to chant your name, *his mother's name*, in the *Dirge Common to the Cathedral Henge of Eileen the Immortal*."

Turn the page for a preview chapter of the next book in The Assassins of Harmony series, *The Chosen of the Generations*.

ONE

The chieftain's magus told him, and the telling silenced the echoes of the victim's screams.

The chieftain was Vernon, the ruler of Clan Innes-Martin.

He said that he had already learned about the cancer that was stalking him, that was hollowing him out from the inside, slow but sure. He asked again about his sons.

Vernon's magus stared up at him, now openly confused.

He shouldn't have been.

Vernon's question had been clear enough: Which of my sons will succeed me?

And yet, his magus looked like a man trapped between the waking world and the world of trance, unable to tell one from the other.

For its part, the waking world was plain enough. The victim's blood was red and glistened in the torchlight. It dripped from the magus's hands and pattered down onto the pavements. The hot stench of it hovered like a wraith in the air about them.

"Which of my sons is to be chieftain after me?" Vernon demanded, repeating the question, driving home each word as though he were wielding a sledgehammer. Which of them would prove to be the Chosen of the Generations?

Yes, it was his sons who were the cause of this shamanic exercise, not his own health or the lack of it. It was their destinies that had brought Vernon, his magus, the vision dancer, and the victim into the center of the manor's henge, alone and in the middle of the night.

Yes, it was his darling sons, each inept in his own way, that were the reason why the victim's blood now coursed across the slab and drained away into the blood jar.

They were insufferable, the pair of them.

In time...but he was nearly out of time.

The magus nodded and resumed his search.

The victim's screams, now redoubled, knifed through the sacred space and echoed from the Guardians, that double ring of gray-black monoliths that formed the perimeter of the clan's henge. The victim had volunteered, but his willingness did nothing to lessen his screams, his agony.

Vernon forced his heart to close. He had no choice, no possibility of compassion. Too many lives dangled like fish in a gillnet for him to take pity now, either on the victim, or on himself, or on his sons.

Vernon and the magus had bound the victim by his hands, chest, hips, and legs to the slab, but he thrashed despite the leather straps. His eyes gaped in horror, and his neck muscles pulsed like halyards in a windstorm on the Columbia River.

The vision dancer edged closer, eager to play her part.

"I must expose his kidneys," the magus said, and set to work with a different kind of knife.

The victim clenched his teeth on his gag. He succeeded in muffling his screams but not in silencing them. The muscles along his jaws bulged. Could it be that he thought that if he did not cry out, he would, possibly, assure his place among the Gods and the Generations?

After long seconds, the magus announced, "There they are, my lord, the man's kidneys." His expression and his voice were sharper than they had been, as though the waking world had at long last reclaimed him. "It is now for you to choose between them. Which is to be Gregory, and which is to be Bevan? Please point them out."

Vernon's sense of dread billowed up, like the flames and smoke from a pot of burning pitch. He had known that this moment of necessity would come, but now that it was upon him, oh, how he loathed it! Two sons:

two kidneys. Clarity. He sought refuge in an absurd demand for clarity. "What are you talking about?"

"At this stage, only that you must choose, my lord," his magus said. "Which kidney is which son?"

Coming from another man, the words would have been insolent, but from him, they were a bland statement of the inescapable, a reminder of a chieftain's duty, an unnecessary lecture on the ontological identity at the heart of this particular augury, a specific case of a general principle.

The muscles across Vernon's shoulders and up the back of his neck tightened. Was it his own sense of dread that was desiccating his mouth or was it loathing? Faith is easy to come by in the good times, but it must be fought for in the bad. "It is for the Generations to choose, not me."

"No, my lord, it is in fact for *you* to choose. You must point them out. Which kidney is the elder of your sons and which is the younger?"

Which indeed?

Avatars, living metaphors, animated signs, participating symbols, the unification of symbol and reality: these were the means by which the Gods and the Generations gave discourse upon their creation.

Whom was Vernon about to damn, and whom was he about to bless? Blindly!

No, he could not choose blindly.

"What have you found?" Vernon demanded. His voice reverberated from the encircling monoliths.

Despite the force of his demand, the truth was that Vernon had had no choice but to pick blindly. The whole integrity of the augury depended on it.

"Without your answer, my lord, I have laid bare two kidneys and not the future of your house." His voice betrayed his growing impatience.

Magi and augurs—augurs especially, that special breed of magus, like the one now plying his trade before him, with clear eyes and bloodstained hands, a knife poised in his fingers—how Vernon hated them! The bastards ought to have stuck to the flight of birds and to have left the guts of animals and men alone. Come to that, they ought to have left the futures of men alone.

Insisting, the magus added, "My lord, you must answer or the victim will have suffered for nothing."

For nothing? No, Vernon couldn't allow that to happen, nor could he shrink away to die in peace. He had to choose, and so he did. "The left one, then," Vernon said, damning one son and blessing the other. "Let the kidney on the left be Gregory."

But damned to what? And blessed how?

"No, my lord, a verbal answer alone will not do. You must also point, physically. There must be no confusion, no chance of error." He demonstrated, pointing his index finger at a random spot in the victim's viscera. "The procedure is most strict."

Vernon's anger broke cover. "I'm not here to be lectured!"

"No, you're not, my lord. However, your anger will solve nothing. You *must* choose."

Vernon clenched his teeth, stifling his rage and his fear. He pointed at the kidney on his left. "That one," he said. "Let that one be Gregory."

The magus smiled, ever so slightly. They had breached the impasse; they could move on. In the end, the victim's agony had been to some purpose, and perhaps, possibly, it had been to some worthwhile purpose into the bargain.

The magus said, "And thus Bevan is to be the kidney on our right."

"Yes, yes. So and blessed let it be!"

The magus searched more intently. The victim shrieked.

Half speaking aloud and half muttering to himself, the magus said, "That is consistent, my lord, your choice. It tallies with what I've found so far."

Amid a new eruption of the victim's blood and screams, the magus excised the kidneys and laid them in a shallow basin, the left to the left, the right to the right, Gregory and Bevan, side by side.

The magus put aside the knife and handed Vernon's sons to their father.

The victim made a violent, spluttering sound, gagging on his own blood, hacking it up. He thrashed from side to side.

The ropes binding him to the slab tore into his flesh.

Suddenly, his body went rigid, and then he gasped and died.

He made a final, hideous, guttural sound.

Nothing in Vernon's memory equaled it: not his wife's death rattle, not the cries of his soldiers dying in battle, not the shrieks of the condemned, not the shocked screams of the men he'd slain.

The dancer withdrew the blood jar from its place beneath the slab and carried it across the circuit to the altar. She invoked the God of Sight and poured the blood into the sacred fire.

The blood hissed in the flames and spread across the burning wood. A plume of steam and gray smoke billowed up. The unburned blood ran down the altar stones and soaked into the earth.

Nothing was lost.

With her arms spread wide in supplication, the dancer lifted her eyes toward the rising smoke.

She had inscribed her naked body with the signs of the God of Sight, and at His direction, she called His name.

The light of the sacred fire purified the markings on her skin and gave them life.

She smashed the blood jar and began the vision dance.

The warm, sweet smell of death rose from the two kidneys.

The magus turned to them, repeating his inspection.

The tumor on the left, on Gregory, was now unmistakable.

"Your designated heir is diseased, my lord, not physically, perhaps, but no less seriously," the magus said. "If Gregory inherits, he will consume your house and bring death to Clan Innes-Martin."

Vernon had hoped that this time, with this magus and with this technique, the result would be different, that the Gods and the Generations would have relented.

They had not.

Vernon's imagination returned to the pot of burning pitch he'd thought about just moments ago. Its flames and its black smoke reared up like an angry stallion. It pawed the air with steel-shod hooves.

Vernon sighed but refused to let his shoulders sag. How many times before had he heard this same result?

Enough to know its truth.

Enough to accept the hateful necessities it imposed.

Enough not to descend into weeping at the prospect.

Further evasion was impossible, and further delay would only serve to damn his people to servitude and slavery.

"He will consume it in the same way that my tumor is consuming me," Vernon said, still hoping that he was wrong, that he had misunderstood. "Piece by piece, hour by hour."

"Indeed, he will, my lord."

"He is like a cancer, then, in the clan's body."

"Yes, my lord. No other conclusion is possible."

"So Bevan is to be my heir."

"Yes, my lord. There can be no mistake. Bevan will rule after you. He is the Chosen of the Generations."

Vernon handed the kidneys, his two sons, back to the magus.

"How long do I have?"

"More than a year but less than two." The magus left a pause, then added, "In part, you will keep yourself alive until you choose to die."

A spark of hope flared across Vernon's mind, streaking like a shooting star across a dark sky. His physicians had not told him that, had not told him that he could choose, even *in part*. Was maneuver, then, genuinely possible? Could he force himself to stay alive long enough to set things right?

On the far side of the manor henge, the dancer's vision had taken full possession of her. Sweat streamed down her body, and her arms and legs flew in a wild pattern but not in a senseless frenzy. Each move, each sweep of her arms, each undulation of her torso, each leap and kick had pattern and meaning.

Vernon read the dance, but he revealed nothing of what he saw.

Aloud, he said, "Gregory must not be murdered."

"No, my lord," his magus said, "but if he lives, there will be a civil war."

"If Bevan succeeds me as he is, he will bring slaughter and chaos."

"The Generations—"

"Hush," Vernon said. "You weary me."

He sought to glimpse the stars, the Fires of Heaven, but beyond the Moon's precincts, the night was black. The clouds had gathered, settling thick and, for a time, immovable.

"A way will be found," Vernon said, and left yet another silence.

Showing more wisdom than he possessed, his magus did not fill it.

At length, filling it himself, Vernon said, "Never fear. Gregory *shall* die."

The dancer shrieked and dropped to her knees. Her circlet, a tracery of gold and jewels about her head, gleamed in the firelight. She raked her nails across her breasts. Blood flowed from the gashes. She swayed from side to side, still locked in the dance. She keened "The Lament for the Battle Fallen."

The hymn passed between the Guardians and faded into the profane world.

"And his marriage?" his magus asked.

How had he dared such a question?

No matter. It deserved an answer.

"It will go forward as announced," Vernon said, "at the Feast of Mabon."

"To what end, my lord?"

How eager his magus was for blood. "To the end that I have given my word."

"Certainly, my lord."

Was there no end to the man's condescension?

Vernon pointed at the dancer. "Hers is the voice of a dirge singer."

"She'll be glad for your approval."

What an ephemeral thing approval was! "Will she remember the vision she has danced?"

"She might, my lord. Once in a great while, it happens. I assure you it's quite rare."

Vernon approached the dancer, his magus at his side.

The "Lament" died, and the dancer stared up into Vernon's face. Tears and blood lined her cheeks, and in her eyes, he could read the vision she had danced.

Were anyone but Vernon and his magus to see it there, the death of his house and the scattering of his clan would surely follow. The Innes-Martins as a clan would disappear.

In the fluttering of the torches and in the hissing of the altar fire, the Generations of his house cried out to him. They commanded him to silence the dancer, to strike her down, even though she had never spoken in the past.

And yet, she *might* speak in the future: an innocent slip of the tongue, a non-answer that revealed everything, or perhaps to save herself from torture or to save another. She was innocent, but the Generations condemned her. Nothing is of greater danger than innocence.

Answering their call, Vernon—Chieftain of Clan Innis-Martin, Lord of the Five Rivers, Warden of the Seven Lakes, Guardian of the Northern March, Beloved of the Sun, the Earth, the Moon, and of all the Gods, and the Chosen of the Generations—drew his sword, and with one blow, he took her head.

Her blood sprayed into the air from the stump of her neck, and her body collapsed onto the paving stones.

He ended the stroke with the blade of his katana held to the side of his magus' neck.

The man's body stiffened, and his eyes widened in shock. His dismay and his fear were plain. A trickle of the dancer's blood ran from Vernon's steel and stained the collar of the man's cloak.

"You will tell no one what happened here," Vernon said, hitting each word. "You will hold your tongue."

"Yes, my lord. I will never speak of it."

"Do not serve me ill in this!"

"No, my lord," his magus said. But then he relaxed. "You have my word." He was too sure of his own importance, too sure that his status as a magus protected him.

The old fool's glibness angered the chieftain of Clan Innes-Martin.

Vernon twitched his blade and opened a shallow cut in the man's neck. He could have just as easily slit his throat.

His magus yelped.

Vernon said, "You bleed, and yet I live!"

The ancient taboo stated that to draw the blood of a magus was to invite death.

Vernon deepened the cut. The man's blood poured down.

The man's eyes were huge with terror.

Perhaps the Gods and the Generations had not struck Vernon down on the spot because he was already dying, and, therefore, wasn't worth bothering about. Why kill a dead man? Why not allow the cancer to do its work? Death now would be a mercy, and so they would withhold it.

That, surely, was their game. The Gods and the Generations were nothing if not seekers of balance.

Vernon's thoughts turned again.

What if the Gods and the Generations simply didn't care?

It was a fascinating idea.

Had his looming death suddenly and unexpectedly freed him from the old superstitions? Was he finally at liberty to disobey? He worked the edge of his sword still deeper into the magus' flesh.

"Shall I put you to the great test?" Vernon asked. He held the blade motionless, the pressure constant, underscoring the importance of his question.

His magus whimpered and shuddered, but then, by an evident act of will, he suppressed both until he stood mute, trembling as though chilled.

Fool or not, he had some reserves of dignity and skill. What the man had done had taken both will and courage, and such were worthy of reward.

Vernon eased his blade away.

"I think not," Vernon said. "I want your silence, not your death, and Bevan will need you when he rules."

But could Bevan *rule*, or would he descend into a stream of endless daydreams and equally endless tantrums when none of the dreams transformed themselves into realities?

Vernon flicked the blood from his sword and strode away. As he neared the Guardians, that permeable boundary between eternity and the temporal realm, he turned and looked back.

His magus was daubing at the wound on his neck and would not look at him, would not meet his gaze.

But the dancer, her eyes shining as though her severed head were yet alive, unashamed and unafraid, met her chieftain's gaze.

He smiled at her, and from the pavement at the base of the altar, she smiled back at him, content!

About the Author

Jamie McNabb writes in several genres, but concentrates on science fiction and fantasy. His work appears in the *Universe Between*, *Past Crimes*, *Pulse Pounders*, *Valor*, and other issues of *Fiction River*, as well as in a variety of online and print publications.

Jamie has sailed extensively on the Columbia and Willamette rivers, where *The Assassins of Harmony* series takes place.

For further information and to subscribe to his newsletter, please visit his website: www.jamicmcnabb.com or go to https://landing.mailerlite.com/webforms/landing/w7k8s7.